Murder at the Tudor Court

A historical mystery

Mariella Moretti
Colin Sowden

London, 1536. A personal servant of Anne Boleyn's is found dead in the Palace of Whitehall, his skull and face smashed in. From that moment the murderer's final days run parallel to those of the unfortunate Queen.

Contents

Characters: see page 209

Places: see page 214

Prologue. London, Newgate Prison   9

A dangerous mission   12

"These are difficult times."   16

Lady Constance   20

Margery is furious   24

At the scene of the crime   27

The body disappears   30

First night meeting   33

Finally a clue   37

A hint of damp, the smell of decay, silence   40

The secret passage   44

"They say that she was very beautiful."   46

"I realize she is afraid."   50

First questionings   54

A treasure hunt   57

Margery investigates   62

A poisoned goblet   65

A trip on the Thames   67

Lady Alice   70

A delicate young lady   74

'Ring-a-ring-of-roses.'   78

Sir Thomas' night   82

"The tapestry slowly moved…"   84

A bundle of letters   90

In the Queen's rooms   92

The tragedy   97

"Perhaps he'll send her to the stake."   100

"I was condemned to live…"   103

5

"So she will be tried."   107

"Short, fat, old and bleary eyed…"   110

That Simon Barefoot   115

Philip's torment   116

"If you only knew."   120

For the king's pharmacy   123

Where was the letter hidden?   127

"They'll all be executed."   129

"I have nothing more to say…"   132

"Peine forte et dure"   135

"Without any proof?"   138

"She's called Nan Chetwood."   141

Death by water   144

"Accusations against you, anonymous."   147

"Norfolk mustn't know."   150

"The verdict had already been decided…" 153

"Guilty," they all said,
one after the other."   158

Newgate Prison   161

"So you are guilty?"   164

"Do you plead guilty or not guilty?"   168

"Robert Kytchyn, a charlatan!"   171

'If in doubt, say nothing.'   175

An accidental death   178

"We would be all risking our necks ..."   182

"So, she is to die..."   184

"Devoured by rats, mired in mud."   187

Rendezvous at Billingsgate   190

Nightmares   193

"I have come here to die..."   196

A fatal misunderstanding.
Billingsgate wharf   202

Epilogue. England thirty years later   206

Characters   209

Places   214

Primary and secondary sources   217

About the authors   222

Acknowledgements   223

Prologue

London, Newgate Prison
17th May, 1536

On the night of the twenty-third of April 1536, William Crooks, a member of Queen Anne Boleyn's entourage, had been found dead in the Palace of Whitehall, his skull smashed. Now, in the dim light of a Newgate dungeon, a figure could be seen kneeling before a friar – a grey cloak over the shoulders, the hood lowered over the face – making a final confession, seeking forgiveness. The execution would take place some days after.

"That Crooks had followed me along the corridor", said the voice. "Drunk, in a rage. I had nothing to defend myself with."

The voice almost broke at the memory. "Go on," the friar had urged.

In the silence of the cell, water could be heard trickling down the walls. Sewer rats scurried across the floor; huge cockroaches crawled through the filthy straw, from which arose a foul stench of faeces and urine.

"I remembered that in the hall I would find a candlestick, one of the heavy kind. A weapon of defence..." the voice continued.

"Did you manage to grab it?"

"No. Before I could do so, he kicked open the door of one of the rooms along the corridor, pushed me inside, and grasped me by the throat. I leant forward and butted him in the stomach. He staggered back. I reached for a candlestick which I knew would be on one of the chests, and brought it down on his head: once, twice, three times. I could feel the metal penetrating his skull. The man fell to the floor and did not move again."

The cries of prisoners came from nearby cells: clearly some were being tortured. At Newgate, the most brutal prison in the realm, were held vicious killers, men who had murdered their own wives, mothers who had suffocated their children whilst they slept. From that place prisoners only emerged either dead or on the carts which would take them to the gallows at Tyburn.

Yet, reflected the friar, this person seeking absolution is different from the others here: this one speaks gently, the voice seems reconciled rather than defiant.

"What happened next?" he asked.

"I bolted the door and climbed through the window. In one bound I was down on the lawn below."

"No-one saw you? You ran away?"

"I stayed crouched down and listened. The grass was still wet but it had stopped raining. The sound of music and voices came from the Queen's rooms; there, on the river bank, it was very quiet – just the sound of a fountain nearby. I washed my face and hands, which were covered in blood. I could hear the crunch of the gravel as I headed away. There was no one around as I walked and re-entered by a side door. This confession occurred on 17 May 1536, about a month after the murder of William Crooks.

A dangerous mission

Cambridge, Pembroke College
24 April 1536

It was already late afternoon when a horseman, accompanied by a squire, galloped through the narrow streets of Cambridge, still glistening from the rain, and arrived at the entrance to Pembroke College.

"Sir Nicholas Sherman," he squire had announced.

The rider had dismounted. "I bring orders for your dean, Sir Robert Kytchyn," he had said. "I come on behalf of Lord Thomas Howard, Duke of Norfolk."

At the mention of the name of Norfolk a shadow of fear had crossed the doorkeeper's face. He had promptly made way for the visitor, who hastened across the college garden, silent at that time of day.

Through a window which overlooked the courtyard, Sir Nicholas could see a small school room with a low ceiling and beams, where several students were sitting around their master: Sir Robert Kytchyn, the very man he was seeking and who, at that moment, was pointing at pictures on a straw-coloured parchment. Some words reached Sir Nicholas: "So, you see, when the following humours – blood, phlegm, yellow bile and black bile – combine in various ways in somebody…."

Sir Robert was about fifty years old, showing some signs of age in his appearance: the grey hair, curly and rather dishevelled; the waist beginning to bulge; a pair of small, horn-rimmed glasses, which gave his blue eyes an owl-like appearance. He had been born poor, in the village of Girton. As a child he had seen his father thrown into prison on various occasions for having poached deer in the king's forests. In the village, the education of local boys had been entrusted to Benedictine monks, who had encouraged him to continue his studies. In time Robert had become a doctor of such skill that he was knighted by the king, and was recognized as an investigator of criminal matters so adept that he was frequently called to London by the Court of the King's Bench in order to give his opinion on difficult cases.

When Sir Nicholas entered the small room, he seemed to fill it with his presence. Sir Robert's face brightened. "My old friend," he exclaimed, embracing him. He turned to face his students: "We studied here together, we have known each other a very long time."

"We used to go rowing together, and on more than one occasion your master hit me on the head with his oar," said Sir Nicholas.

The young men laughed and Sir Robert replied: "But as you see, Sir Nicholas survived my clumsiness and is now an important figure at the court in London. Well, gentlemen, you can go; we have finished for today."

Like Sir Robert, Sir Nicholas came from a poor village – Longstanton, near Cambridge, where he had proceeded to study with the help of several scholarships. He had then joined the Duke of Norfolk's household as a gentleman-at-arms, fighting with him against Scottish raiders. At Cambridge he had already been tall and well-built, and he had now become even more solid, a real soldier, with a hard face that seemed carved out of wood. 'Perhaps over the years his heart has hardened too?' wondered Sir Robert, when he had met him the previous evening at the royal banquet: in the war the duke's orders had been pitiless – no prisoners to be taken, the outlaws to be put to the sword and their bodies left hanging on trees for all to see, until the whole area stank of death.

When the two men were alone, Sir Nicholas collapsed on a bench: only then did Sir Robert notice that his friend's cloak and boots were covered in mud, and his face displayed signs of extreme exhaustion.

"I come directly from Hampton Court, where the court has taken refuge. An epidemic has broken out in London."

"The plague again?"

"This time it's the sweating sickness."

"I know it. It arrived with us some years ago. All of a sudden people started dropping to the ground: a high temperature, vile-smelling sweat, death in a matter of hours."

"Well, that's what is happening in London at the moment. The capital is deserted, streets are blocked off, the city is rotting. The markets – Cheapside, Billingsgate – are empty. Those who are still alive carry away their dead, in wagons, carts, even wheelbarrows. They pile them in heaps and take them to be burnt outside the city walls. The fires illumine the sky all night."

Sir Robert took a large jug of beer from a recess in the wall, removed the cover and filled a pewter cup. He handed this to his friend, who promptly drained it, heaved a sigh and wiped his mouth with his sleeve. "But I am not here to talk about what is happening in London. I have a message for you regarding the Queen – a commission, personal and secret."

"Oh no, Nicholas."

"Don't worry. It is Anne Boleyn's uncle himself who has entrusted you with the task."

"You mean the Duke of Norfolk."

"In person, I am one of his gentlemen of the bedchamber."

Instantly Sir Robert sprang up, as if bitten by a snake: "Nicholas," he whispered, "Wait a minute."

"These are difficult times."

Cambridge, Pembroke College
24 April 1536

"Just a minute."

Sir Robert went to the door and looked out, making sure that there was no-one lurking in the corridor. Returning to his seat, he murmured: "These are difficult times, even the walls have ears." In truth he was already dismayed at the thought of a commission which might take him away from the peaceful routine of his studies, and the mere mention of the intrigues of Court made him uneasy.

If Sir Nicholas was aware of this, he did not show it. Instead, he produced from under his waistcoat a folded parchment carrying the seal of the Duke of Norfolk, and handed it to Robert. "This document gives you all the authority that you will need."

At his friend's invitation, the visitor poured himself some more beer, then started to explain: "This is what happened: yesterday a certain William Crooks, that the King had imposed on the Queen as a close servant — in fact to spy on her — was found dead in a room at the royal palace of Whitehall. His head had been smashed in. He was a dishonest character. There had been rumours about him being involved in blackmail, that he knew something about the Queen and had her in his power. And now the Queen herself fears for her life. This is where you come in."

"But how do I come into it?"

"There will be an inquest, and the Duke has appointed you his official coroner."

"Oh, no, not me!"

"I am afraid so. The Duke described to the king several cases which you have solved: that of the sudden disappearance of the Lord Mayor of Bury St Edmund's, whom everyone believed dead, and that you, making enquiries among your various county connections, discovered performing with a group of actors travelling around Lincolnshire."

A pause as if to recollect. "And the case of the Ely cleric, found murdered in the cell of a young nun in a convent in Norfolk. And something to do with a baker in Bosworth. I don't know the details."

"Ah, yes, the baker of Bosworth," recalled Sir Robert, smiling. "I remember that case well, it was two years ago. There was an old man who, it appeared, had been stung to death by wasps: his body was black and swollen and covered in stings. The wife and her young friend, a sailor from Portsmouth, had given their testimonies: 'We found him early in the morning, in the courtyard; there was nothing we could do'. They had both sworn to this. But in Leicestershire that year it had been hard winter, with snow storms and thick ice: it was highly unlikely that so many of the insects had survived."

"So the bailiff of Market Bosworth asked you assist him in his investigation."

"Indeed, and on examining the body I noticed that there were marks on his wrists and ankles, abrasions, which suggested that the man had been strung up on ropes."

"The sailor from Portsmouth…"

"I examined the stings, which were all identical, in a regular pattern, almost like a piece of embroidery. I realized that they must have pricked him with needles dipped in the sap of some poisonous plant."

"A grim death."

"Terrible, poor man. But in the end, the two of them confessed."

"Norfolk must have been told about it. He is the King's advisor, so the sovereign will have heard too. He has decided that you are the right man to lead this enquiry, and he wants you at Whitehall immediately."

Sir Robert raised his hands as if in a gesture of surrender. "Nicholas, I am nearly forty years old. Don't you see that I'm almost an old man."

"And so?"

"I am a countryman at heart. I always feel uncomfortable at court. Besides, I have responsibilities here: my students, my wife…"

"You will be able to take her with you, and a couple of servants, and whatever else you need. You will be lodging at Hampton Court, but in the morning you and I will make our way down the river to London, and will spend the day at Whitehall, to begin our investigation." He then added: "You cannot refuse, the King has commanded it. And we must hurry, before the clues disappear."

"And the body, where is it?"

"I haven't had it moved." Sir Nicholas took a final mouthful of beer, then: "So let us go to your house, if you don't mind. I shall tell you the rest over dinner."

'The rest? Whatever else will he have to say to me?' wondered Sir Robert.

Lady Constance

Cambridge, Fair Street
24 April 1536

By the time that they arrived at Sir Robert's house, the rain had stopped and the deep vermillion of its brick walls shone radiantly in the setting sun. Dismounting, Sir Nicholas shielded his eyes with his hand. "The swallows are flying high. We shall have good weather tomorrow," observed Sir Robert.

Surrounding the house – a two-storey building with a sundial painted in blue on the south-facing side – was a well-cared-for garden, with beds of roses, purple clematis climbing trellises on the walls and boxwood hedges, all of which exhaled a rich scent in the evening air. Barrels of water stood in the corners, kept there to warm in the sun before being used on the garden. From one of the ground-floor windows glimmered the faint light of a candle.

Lady Constance, Sir Robert's wife, Sir Nicholas and Sir Robert dined together with the easy familiarity of old friends who had not seen each other for some time. Constance followed the men's exchanges with a youthful smile on her face. She was taller than her husband by a span, green eyes flecked with gold, a determined nose, slim in a dress of cream-coloured brocade, which was elegant but a little worn at the sleeves, with a headdress of the same colour, under which was tucked her bright red hair. She came from the old Kentish nobility, and before getting married had been a maid of honour to the king's first wife, Catherine of Aragon. Beautiful and high-born as she was, Constance could have aspired to a distinguished marriage. But she had fallen in love with Robert Kytchyn, at that time a young master at Cambridge.

No army of retainers to look forward to, no feasts on a splendid large estate, no chance of playing the lady of the manor: now she was merely a wife who managed a small household, who wove, who cooked, who supervised the kitchen and the production of beer. Yet a woman who was happy. And because she was shrewd and had sharp intuition, she had often assisted in her husband's investigations when he had been entrusted with a delicate task by one of the courts of law.

The table was laid in a small room panelled with dark oak, the well-polished pewter plates resplendent against the pure white table cloth, whilst in the fireplace a gentle blaze kept away the evening damp. The dinner consisted of a tasty soup of leeks done in milk, various stewed vegetables, fish fresh from the river in a thick spicy sauce, followed by a pudding flavoured with cinnamon.

Sir Nicholas recalled the wedding of Lady Constance and Sir Robert, fifteen years previously, at Cambridge, in the little round church of the Holy Sepulchre, which was bedecked with flowers from the surrounding countryside. He had been witness for his friend. "You had become acquainted at court, I seem to remember."

"I was in London for a consultation. I was awkward and unpolished. Constance was a lady-in-waiting to good Queen Catherine, and she was very beautiful."

She smiled: "There had been a great dinner, at which the King and Queen had presided, and I had found myself sitting next to him," continued Lady Constance. "While everyone was talking, enjoying themselves, he was silent, embarrassed, just looking at me all the time, and when I returned his gaze he just looked down."

"After the meal came the dances. But I did not know how to dance, so I remained silent, staring at her."

"I joined in all the dances, though, and when the evening was over I retired with the other ladies. Some of them started making fun of me: 'You've certainly impressed that young man from Cambridge,' they said. 'Me? But he did not speak a word to me the whole time we were together.' Would you believe it? A few months later we became betrothed and married soon after."

"And do you remember," said Sir Nicholas, helping himself to some more wine, "the ceremony in which you were knighted by King Henry?"

"It was because Robert had saved Queen Anne's life at the birth of Princess Elizabeth. He never mentions it, but that was the reason," Lady Constance said. Her voice became hesitant: "Tell me, Sir Nicholas, is it true that she is now out of favour?"

"After the last miscarriage, in January. It was dreadful."

"It's a terrible thing to lose a child," murmured Lady Constance. Five years previously they too had had a child: a vigorous little boy, who kicked when being changed, who yelled at the top of his voice when he wanted feeding. Born in January, in June a fever had carried him off. She had almost died in the birth, and since then no more children had come.

"But in this case it's different. It became rumoured that the Queen had had relations with gentlemen of the court, as people doubted that the King was still capable of fathering an heir."

"And to think that he was called 'The Great Harry, the handsomest man in Christendom'," said Lady Constance.

"Now he is grown huge, with a mound of a stomach, the wound on his leg threatening to turn gangrenous and smelling so vile that it is hard to stay close to him."

"After the miscarriage, the King, how did he react?" asked Lady Constance.

"From that moment on the King and Queen only appeared together on official occasions, but he no longer shared her bed."

Margery is furious

Cambridge, Fair Street
24 April 1536

Lady Constance rose promptly from the table: the departure for London was to be on the following day, immediately after the bells announced the first offices of the day, Matins and Lauds. "I shall take my governess with me. While I am with the court ladies, seeking to learn something from them, Margery can listen to the gossip in the servants' hall and the marketplace."

"An excellent idea: dear old Margery, a real grumbler, but good at getting people to talk," agreed Sir Nicholas.

"And with me must come Philip, my assistant," said Sir Robert. "Philip Glover. A good lad. You'll like him. He was entrusted to my care by his mother, a widow of these parts, so that I might make a doctor of him. He's respectful, affectionate. Studious, but also something of a dreamer. He plays the lute and composes songs. And he's even a little in love with my spouse."

Lady Constance blushed, shot a disapproving glance at her husband and hurriedly left the room.

"I wonder what we shall find in the city?" Lady Constance commented later, when they were alone and she, in front of the mirror, was combing out her hair, before plaiting it in tresses for the night. "When I looked for Margery in order to make the final arrangement for the journey, I found her scolding the scullery-boy. She was in a real temper over our leaving. She says that the streets of London stink of dung, that nobody thinks twice about emptying a chamber pot on your head from the window above, that the cobbles are so filthy that you can't keep your feet…"

"…and that thieves and murderers spring out at every corner, and that you can die of hunger before anyone will offer you a crust of bread. She never misses an opportunity to complain, but she would squawk like a chicken if you proposed going by yourself."

Sir Robert got into bed. "You, though: are you sure that you want to come? With all that's happening in London, it could be dangerous this time."

"I'm not a stay-at-home, you know that. Whilst you, the learned doctor!" Her eyes sparkled. "Absent-minded and always late. You would not survive a day without me."

Her husband put on his night cap: without his little glasses his face assumed a look of vulnerability which was almost childlike. "Connie, with all the cases that I have dragged you into over the last fifteen years, have you not ever wished yourself rid of me?"

"There have been times, yes," and Lady Constance smiled again, getting into bed herself. She cuddled close to him. He extinguished the last candle.

At the scene of the crime

London, Whitehall Palace
25th April 1536

As soon as Sir Nicholas, Sir Robert and the young Philip had arrived in London, two of the Duke of Norfolk's guards accompanied them to the room where the crime had taken place.

Philip was a tall young man, of slight build and clear complexion, with soft brown eyes and the beginnings of a well-tended beard on his chin. Dignified in the attire that Margery ensured was always clean and tidy, with the collar of his white shirt well starched and an orange velvet jacket with buttons of the same colour, he had been a member of Sir Robert's household for several years. Under the latter's tutelage, Philip promised to become a good doctor one day, even though Margery had on more than one night caught him writing poetry and songs by firelight, a blanket wrapped around his thin shoulders.

A certain Simon Barefoot, assistant to the court doctor, had also inveigled his way into their group. The previous evening Sir Nicholas had spoken about him to his friend: "Where do people like that come from? Certainly not from Oxford. He's always meddling; he would have liked Norfolk to appoint him coroner, but he's just an impertinent fool."

"So why do they keep him on at court?"

"He's got a smooth way of talking – like a prelate, and people are deceived. But he has a knife hidden under his cassock. Beware of him."

Now this Barefoot – an ordinary little man, with white hair, long and straight, eyes red like a mouse, eyebrows as white as the hair, and an unpleasant smell about his person – approached Sir Robert with a servile bow: "I offer you my assistance. You'll find it very useful."

'Presumptuous oaf', thought Sir Robert, replying with a slight nod.

Arriving at the end of a corridor, the group stopped outside a door.

"There's a small panel missing here," noted Sir Robert. "It was taken out by the joiner on the night of the crime so that the bolt inside could be pushed back," said Sir Nicholas. "Yes, whoever was staying in these rooms could not have entered because, oddly, the door had been locked from the inside."

Simon Barefoot rushed forward to play the host. "Here we are. This is the room in which William Crooks was killed. He was a leading figure at court, and a good friend of mine."

All went in, to be met by the stench of death. Crooks' large body was still curled up next to the wooden chest, one arm outstretched, with dried blood and tufts of reddish hair on the smashed skull. On turning him over, they saw that most of the face had been reduced to pulp, with flies crawling round what was left of it, and the one remaining eye staring up as if in surprise.

One of the windows was wide open, and Barefoot reached to open the other. "Stop, don't touch anything," barked Sir Nicholas. And Sir Robert: "On the night of the murder, when you came in, did you move anything?"

"Nobody called me that night."

"So who certified the death?"

"Doctor Butts wasn't at court, so we called Master Bryan, the farrier who sees to the king's horses," said Sir Nicholas.

And looking at Barefoot he shook his head and added: "We trust Bryan."

The body disappears

London, Palace of Whitehall
25 April 1536

Ignoring Barefoot's indignant look, Sir Robert leant over the corpse. "The blood has formed a pool under the chest and coagulated there. The floor slopes in that direction."

"A candle-stick has rolled under there," observed Philip, pointing to a large chest.

While Sir Robert and his assistant examined the body, Simon Barefoot wandered around. He approached the window, picked up the stool beneath and put it under the table. Sir Robert gestured to Sir Nicholas, who grabbed the man by his arm: "How dare you? You were told not to touch anything, you clod!"

Barefoot looked at him shocked. He hesitated, then hurried out of the room.

Sir Robert asked "Are we free of him?"

"I did my best, but we shouldn't fool ourselves."

A blood-covered candlestick lay near the body. Sir Robert picked it up carefully. "A very heavy base," he said. "The murderer must have picked it up by the stem, perhaps with two hands, and then delivered several wild blows. He must have really detested him, to reduce him to this. He struck downwards, so he must be taller than the victim."

"Someone taller than the victim: that rather limits the range of suspects," observed Sir Nicholas, "although, as we can see, Crooks was relatively short."

"We'll have to make a further examination of the corpse, more thorough," said Sir Robert, "but not here."

Sir Nicholas gave orders to the guards: "You can wrap up the body in a sheet now. Put it in a basket and leave it in the coldest part of the cellars, under the stables."

Simon Barefoot stood listening outside, his ear close to the door. "They won't find it easy to keep hold of that body," he muttered to himself, then moved away quickly.

Meanwhile Sir Robert had approached the window. "The murderer escaped through here, given that the door was bolted from the inside. That was a clever move because it delayed discovery. He leant out over the window ledge: He was wearing something crimson. A rich person's material and colour," he noted, and saying this, he removed a thick thread of deep red from the plaster surrounding the window. He handed it to his assistant, who slipped it gently between two pieces of parchment, and then in a small shoulder-bag. He sat down on the edge of the bed, Sir

31

Nicholas and Philip standing in front of him, "There's something that I don't understand," he murmured. "Nicholas, you told me that there was a celebration that night in the palace, something for a few favourites, whose names you wrote down for me. Among these was Crooks; however, no-one seems to have noticed his absence until very late on. How is that possible?"

"There was a treasure hunt. Messages and objects had been hidden in various places around the palace. The guests had to find them and bring them back to the main hall. All this time the music and dancing continued. The crime was only discovered when everyone went to bed, and two of the Queen's ladies couldn't get into their rooms because the door had been locked from the inside."

"Yes, Nicholas, I still fail to understand," said Sir Robert. "Why was that Crooks involved?" And he passed his hand through his hair, as he always did when thinking hard. "Anyway, now we have a more urgent task: to go and see what else our corpse may tell us."

But something strange had happened: when they arrived in the cellars, where the two guards had been told to place Crooks' body, they were baffled: the dead man was nowhere to be found.

First night meeting

**Hampton Court
25 April 1536**

During the journey from Cambridge to Whitehall it had been decided that while Sir Robert, Sir Nicholas and Philip conducted their official enquiries in London, Lady Constance and, in particular, Margery, would talk to as many people as possible in the royal household in order to obtain more information.

Margery was an elderly woman, of such an honest aspect that whoever was with her felt at ease: but between one piece of gossip and another, she always managed to find out what she wanted to know. Then, at the end of each day, the five of them were to get together and report to each other the results of their separate investigations.

And so the five assembled on the first night at court in the beautiful high-ceilinged rooms that had been provided for them in the royal residence of Hampton Court Palace. It was nearly night-time: a few hours previously a banquet had been held in their honour in the great hall, with music and entertainments by the court jesters; then, when the tables had been removed, the dancing had begun. Lady Constance had taken part too: first of all there had been a slow dance followed by a solemn pavane, both with her husband, then some lively galliards with Philip, which had left her red-faced and radiant.

They were sitting around a table on which stood a carafe of wine, sweetened with honey and flavoured with spices, and Sir Robert prepared to give an account of their findings at Whitehall.

"What is the room where the crime was committed like?" asked Lady Constance.

"On the wall there is an Arras tapestry: a knight of the Round Table, I think. Rather faded and threadbare. Then two stools and a small table, two chests, a large canopied bed. It is the room of two ladies-in-waiting to the Queen, perhaps two sisters. The candlestick with which Crooks was killed must have stood on the chest near the door because there are drops of wax on the wood."

"The candle-stick. What was it like?"

"Square, heavy. The candle – made of expensive beeswax – had rolled under the chest."

"Was everything in order?"

"I lifted up the lids of both chests: women's clothes and some dress material inside, all carefully folded away, with little bags of lavender inside."

"Nothing lying around?"

"Some slippers, a bit worn, as you might expect women sleeping alone to wear. But the most astonishing thing is that when Sir Nicholas, Philip and I went down into the cellars, the corpse was not where it should have been. Obviously someone had moved it."

"And who, if not that so-called doctor, that Simon Barefoot who you told us about?" added Lady Constance, who was not entirely unfamiliar with happenings at court.

"If we had stayed to investigate, we would have missed the high tide on the river," explained Sir Nicholas. "We'll do that tomorrow morning. I'll have all the cellars searched, and every other possible hiding-place. I'll make him pay for it, that scoundrel."

"And you, my dear, have you discovered anything?" Sir Robert asked his wife.

"The Queen spoke to me for only a few minutes. Do you remember when we came to London for her coronation? It was in the May, three years ago, the longed-for heir would be born in the September, and the Queen was a truly happy woman, at the side of a beaming monarch. The present Anne Boleyn seems a mere shadow of her former self: withered, embittered. Did you notice, at dinner, the sour look that the King directed towards her? It cannot just be a matter of the miscarriage: there must be something more serious behind it."

"Holy Virgin," murmured Margery, "what could be worse?"

They were silent for a moment. "Will you be able to see her again?" asked Sir Robert eventually.

"She asked me to go to her tomorrow."

"And the little Elizabeth?"

"She's a pretty child: she has the copper-coloured hair of her father, the oval face and dark eyes of her mother. But her expression is sad; I am sure that she realizes that all is not well between her parents."

Finally a clue

Hampton Court
25 April 1536

At those words Sir Robert sighed: "All that is distressing. I remember her being born. The sovereign was certain that it would be a boy, had consulted astrologers and had even prepared scrolls announcing as much to be sent to all the princes of Europe. But difficulties were foreseen and I was called in by the court physician, a former colleague who knew that I had had some experience in similar cases. It was a difficult birth: the Queen was screaming, convinced that we would let her die providing the heir could be preserved. Fortunately, Doctor Butts and I were able to save both mother and child." He passed a hand through his hair: 'It seems a long time ago,' he thought. He turned to the governess. "Margery, have you managed to discover anything else?"

"I've been trying to find out more about William Crooks, but it will take time to win the confidence of the court servants."

"Give the cook the recipe for your cinnamon pudding and all doors will open before you," suggested Sir

Nicholas. The soldier, despite his rough exterior, had a soft spot for Margery and her choice dishes.

"I shall do so, sir," and the old lady's plump face shone with pride. "But now let me tell you what I learnt when I visited the market here today."

"We know that you have a passion for markets and fairs," Sir Robert teased.

"Well, it was worth it. I saw the monks going round with their shoulder bags, and I bought some ointment from one of them, for sore throats. It might be useful here, with this awful air. But they had nothing to tell me about Crooks."

"Too far from court," commented Lady Constance.

"And then," continued Margery, "there were the merchants with their carpets, spices, wool, the craftsmen with loads of pans, knives and lanterns, and farmers selling eggs, vegetables, chickens. One of them had spread out his wares on a cloth on the ground, and then had been fined for grabbing hold of passers-by in order to get their attention."

The others listened, beguiled by her manner of story-telling.

"Anyway, as I was making my way back to the palace, I joined company with one of the cooks and started talking about William Crooks. In order to gain time I walked slowly. I told her that my feet were aching: in fact, I was in some pain. Then I gave her the recipe for the plum sauce, the one that is served with roast meat."

"One of your precious secrets," said Sir Nicholas.

"A very straightforward secret: cinnamon, ginger, almonds and cardamom mashed together. And toasted breadcrumbs and sugar. All simmered in red wine."

"And plums," suggested Lady Constance.

"Yes, and plums. Then you sieve it. That's all," concluded Margery. And continued: "Speaking of Crooks, he was a slimy individual, according to what that woman told me at the end. 'In what way?', I asked casually. 'He ran after all the servant girls, the young ones and even those that were married.' 'That's not done,' I said. And she added 'They say that he was involved in dirty dealings with some rather dishonest folk.' But more than this I could not get her to say."

"At last a clue worth following!" commented Sir Robert. "Well done, our Margery."

Soon the sky would begin to lighten: "Nicholas," said Sir Robert, "Philip and I will leave for London after the morning office. At Whitehall palace we shall search out Crooks' body so I can do a proper examination. Sir Nicholas will be able to question the servants. We shall be back at Hampton Court by evening and may be able to start questioning our first witnesses. For that I'll need your help, Nicholas."

A hint of damp, the smell of decay, silence

London, Palace of Whitehall
26 April 1536

The following morning, in London, Sir Nicholas questioned the men whom he had charged with removing the body. "We placed the basket in the vault next to the stables, as you ordered," they declared. They had eyes swollen from drinking too much and looked ill at ease: it was clear that they were lying.

"How much did Barefoot pay you?" asked Sir Robert brusquely.

"He didn't, sir. He threatened us."

The two men hesitated, about to continue, but Sir Nicholas interrupted: "In what way?"

"He said that he would make known some of the things we had done."

"For example?"

"Well…" Looking down, they did not wish to say any more.

"The body, where is it now? Tell us!" snarled Sir Nicholas.

"He told us to take it to the cellars alongside the river, those that flood at high tide."

They hurried there, the guards pulled out a wicker basket still dripping with water and carried it to a dry vault nearby. They lit some torches on the wall, lifted the body out of the basket, removed the clothes and laid it carefully on a trestle table.

A hint of damp, the smell of decay, silence.

Sir Robert tied a handkerchief around his face, covering his nose and mouth but leaving his eyes exposed. Sir Nicholas and Philip did the same. The three of them approached the table, where a servant was holding a torch.

Sir Robert crossed himself and lent over the corpse, his voice nearly breaking when pronouncing the set formula: "We are called upon to examine this poor body, may God help us!" He continued: "We have here a man of about forty years of age, short, heavily built. A pronounced abdomen, characteristic of someone who eats and drinks a lot. From what is left of his face, we can make out that he had a low forehead, thick eyebrows, a large nose and a double chin. One eye remains, and it is fixed open. The mouth is wide open too, the teeth black and broken. The skull has been smashed, and there is tissue protruding. The few hairs on his head are reddish in colour."

In the silence that followed, there was a muffled scraping, as if of steps, and a sudden draught made the torches flicker. Sir Nicholas murmured: "Someone opened a door, it must be Barefoot. Let's not show that we have noticed anything, and we may catch him."

Sir Robert nodded: "The hairs on the body are reddish too. As we noted before, he has been struck violently on the face and the top of the head with a heavy object, from above, repeatedly. There are no other wounds. Thick, hairy hands, now without rings, although the mark of them can still be seen on the fingers."

"Several rings he had, when you first examined him," Philip pointed out. "And he was wearing a pair of soft leather boots: expensive, I thought."

"Have you taken them?" Sir Nicholas demanded of one of the attendants.

"They were no use to him any more. Nor the rings," was the reply.

"Robbing a corpse! You shall be punished as you deserve," growled Sir Nicholas.

Sir Robert had renewed his examination: "As for the rest of the body, he has thin legs. The feet are flat, deformed; he must have had difficulty walking. No scars that I can see. Even though we know the approximate hour of death, the body has been under water for several hours, which affects its degree of rigidity and the nature of the hypostatic marking."

"What marks?" asked Sir Nicholas.

"The purple marks which form half an hour or so after death in the lower part of the body. They would have given a more precise idea of when he was killed." And he added: "As always happens when I find myself before someone dead, even a rogue as this one was, I feel sad: how were they before now, what dreams did they have, what hopes, what disappointments..."

In the meantime Sir Nicholas had gone up to the door, flung it open and stepped out into the corridor. All he saw was the edge of a dark cloak disappearing round the corner.

The secret passage

London, Whitehall Palace
26 April 1536

In the room which had been placed at his disposal, Sir Robert washed his hands and face in a bowl full of steaming water. He was exhausted and lay down on the bed.

"Have you reached any conclusion?" Philip asked him.

"We shall soon learn more about Crooks, thanks to our Margery. I am convinced that it will be Crooks himself who will lead us to the killer. His dirty dealings – I have asked Nicholas to fully investigate those two scoundrels. Also the rage with which he was killed, are both very indicative. We shall find the motive, and that will help us to…" He had fallen asleep and was snoring. Philip sat down at the table, lay down his head and dozed too. They both jumped up when someone knocked at the door: it was Sir Nicholas. "I had both of those good-for-nothing guards soundly whipped. In the end they talked."

"What had they been doing?

"Apparently Crooks used to steal objects from gentlemen of the court, a jewel here, a cup there, and those two sold them off in some market in the North. They divided the proceeds. At the same time, he implicated a servant girl in the business and blackmailed her into his bed. He was the Queen's factotum, a powerful man at court."

They later returned to where the crime had been committed, examined every corner of the room but did not find anything new. However, on closing the shutters, Philip noticed that the tapestry on the wall in front of the bed moved slightly, as if disturbed by a current of air. He lifted a corner, asked Sir Nicholas to help him, and together they pulled it halfway from the wall. There, behind the tapestry, was concealed a small door.

"They say that she was very beautiful."

Hampton Court
26 April 1536

It was almost evening when Sir Robert, Sir Nicholas and Philip came back from Whitehall, soaked from the rain. At Hampton Court too it had rained all day and Lady Constance had had dinner laid in her own rooms, in front of a roaring fire.

"There are no entertainments at court this evening," she said in a low voice, when all five of them were seated around the table. "The King has left for Wolf Hall, to pay court to that dull Jane Seymour."

"Jane Seymour, do you know her?" asked Sir Robert.

"She was a maid of honour to Anne Boleyn, which is when he fell in love with her. The Queen will be alone in her rooms."

"Have you seen her, the Queen?"

"I spent some time with her this afternoon. She spoke very openly with me. She knows that we are all loyal to her."

Hers was a loyalty which dated back to the old friendship between the Boleyns and Sherbournes: the lands of Lady Constance's father, Sir Edward, weren't far from those of Sir Thomas Boleyn. As children, in the summer sunshine, Anne and Constance had played in the meadows surrounding Hever Castle, together with their brothers and sisters. The two girls had then exchanged letters during the years in which the young Anne was a maid of honour to Queen Claude de Valois-Orléans, and later they were reunited as maids of honour to Queen Catherine of Aragon. So although Anne Boleyn had fallen from favour, the loyalty of Lady Constance remained firm.

"They say that she was very beautiful," observed Philip.

"She certainly was. She had dark eyes and hair, a supple figure, a slender neck and an elegance gained at the French court. She could captivate men with a single glance, and Henry was completely captivated."

"Do you know how her first meeting with the King occurred?" Philip pursued.

"It was at a public audience, she recounted it to me herself. The king was seated on his throne, all in gold, and still very handsome at that time. At his side Cardinal Wolsey was giving out names and details of the various people as they came up in turn to pay homage. 'Lord Henry Percy, Duke of Northumberland, now in my service, and his betrothed, Lady Anne Boleyn,' he murmured into his ear at a certain point.

The king was dazzled by her youthful beauty: 'Tell me more,' he ordered Wolsey.

'She's the daughter of Sir Thomas Boleyn, our ambassador in Paris.'

'Why is she here?'

'She has asked to be accepted among the ladies-in-waiting of your wife, Queen Catherine.'"

"Where it led we all know," said Sir Nicholas. He rose from the table and went over to the window. It had stopped raining, the clouds had gone and the sky was full of stars. "I was already at court by then and I felt that from that moment the history of our kingdom was going to take a very different path. On the same day Wolsey forced Lord Percy to abandon his betrothed and return to his father's estates in the North. He had to marry someone else."

"And the King?" asked Lady Constance.

He began to pay court to the young Anne. She declared that she might be able to love him but 'since my honour is precious to me above all things', she demanded that he divorce his first wife, the Spanish princess, and make her his queen instead."

Sir Robert too stood up and began pacing about the room. "Although we weren't at court, we knew what was happening," he said. "Years of dispute with Rome – the Pope refusing to grant him a divorce – of quarrels with Spain and France, who threatened to invade. Finally, when Lady Anne accepted his advances and became pregnant, the king sent away his first wife. Catherine died of a broken heart in an out-of-the-way castle. The Pope excommunicated him and he in turn broke with the Church of Rome."

"Trials of dissident Catholics followed, beheadings, the plundering of the monasteries, the raping nuns by his soldiers, bonfires of manuscripts. Even at Cambridge they burnt a few, in the market place," added Lady Constance.

"And after seven years of struggle he finally married Anne Boleyn, no longer so young. The ceremony took place in a chapel in Whitehall, in front of a handful of witnesses, one cold early morning in late January. The following September the baby Elizabeth was born," concluded Sir Robert.

Talk stopped while one servant cleared away the dishes from the main courses and another placed on the table carafes of Chablis and plates of variously coloured marzipan sweets.

"Margery Ackworth, these don't compare with your famous puddings," Sir Nicholas teased.

"You may well say so! The airs the cooks give themselves, and the waste in the kitchens! What they steal between them would feed an army! And the dirt and the filth which builds up on the floors: leftovers, droppings and urine from monkeys and dogs all over, in every murky corner…" Margery was disgusted: her double chin trembled in irritation; even her white bonnet had gone awry, revealing a wisp of indignant grey hair.

"I realize she is afraid."

Hampton Court
26 April 1536

No sooner had the servants left the room than Lady
Constance continued what she had been saying: "The
Queen is a good mother. She has shown me the
clothes that she has embroidered for the little
Elizabeth, and the pretty dolls that she sews for her.
But she's grown old before her time; her face has
become drawn and her skin dry, and she's lost that
rather superior air that she used to have. She told me
of her miscarriage, and I could see that she was afraid.
'When the King wanted to divorce Catherine, well, it
wasn't easy for him,' she told me. 'She was a princess
of Aragon, and the English loved her. He put her away
in a remote castle, and it killed her. I am not a king's
daughter, at court and beyond I have no-one to
defend me, to them all I'm just a slut who stole away
another woman's husband.'
'Your Grace...' I started to say.
'For months I was spied upon, this is something I'm
sure you're not aware of. By an awful fellow, a certain

William Crooks, the one that was found dead in Whitehall a few nights ago.'

'That's what Sir Robert is investigating at the moment,' I said.

'He had come creeping up to me one day 'By order of the sovereign' he had said. Insistent, persuasive: 'I shall be your servant, always at your side.' I didn't understand, and he added 'To protect you, my lady. There are many slanders circulating about you', and he winked at me slyly, with his snake's eyes. 'Slanders that I could report here at court,' he insinuated. 'The fine gentlemen that surround you, with whom you dance, on which particular occasions...' Thus he blackmailed me, he wanted money, more and more.'

'Do you think he'll denounce you to the sovereign?' I asked.

'I'm certain of it. I think that Henry is tired of me. He's concocting one of his schemes. He'll dispose of me, have me shut up in a convent. And I have a feeling that it will be soon.' "

Margery rose to put another log on the fire. The flames leapt, sending sparks into the dark chimney. Lady Constance gave orders for the servants to clear the table and to place chairs and a bench by the hearth. At a sign from Sir Robert, she bolted the door. They all sat around the fire.

"I have a piece of news," said Sir Robert to the two women. "I didn't mention it before because I was not sure of its importance. Well, this morning, as we were inspecting the room where the crime had taken place, we discovered a secret passage."

Immediately Sir Nicholas and Philip joined him in explaining what had happened, interrupting each other excitedly, like boys recounting an adventure. Sir Robert began: "Well, one of us moves aside the tapestry, and there behind it we find a door: small, but strong, made of oak. We look at each other: what further horror might it conceal? Is it a trap?"

Sir Nicholas continued the story: "Philip runs to lock the room by throwing the bolt, so that no-one can come in and play a trick on us. We help by pushing a bench against the door."

"So we go to the tapestry door, turn the handle, it opens without a sound: the hinges are well oiled, so it has obviously been used recently. But not by the murderer, who we know escaped through the window."

"Unless he had deliberately stuck that red woollen thread that you found on the window frame, in order to lead you astray, and then had indeed escaped via the passage," remarked Lady Constance quietly.

"True, my dear, an interesting theory to bear in mind," replied Sir Robert, reflecting that once again his wife had hit the mark. "Anyway," he continued, "we throw wide the door and find that it opens onto a passageway of beaten earth. It's narrow, dark and stinks of mould. We have to decide what to do, we debate for a few minutes, and agree to go on. We file into the tunnel, Sir Nicholas leading the way, bent almost double, with Philip holding a candlestick, and me bringing up the rear."

"The passageway seems to go on for ever," continued Philip. "We make our way slowly, with effort. At a certain point a sudden draft blows out the candle. 'Damnation!' I cry. We carry on in the dark, groping our way with our hands, brushing along the walls, and in the silence all we can hear was our breathing."

Lady Constance and Margery listened with baited breath. And Sir Robert: "All of a sudden we come upon a flight of stairs, nearly breaking our necks in the process."

Sir Nicholas continues: "We go down a few steps until, after another bend, it starts to get lighter, and there is something gleaming in the distance."

Then Philip: "We can hear voices and there arrives the smell of food cooking."

"We reach a door, half-closed."

"We look through the gap and can see the kitchen fires, and cooks, and young half-naked scullery boys bustling about between the cauldrons."

"We don't show ourselves, but decide to retrace our steps and to keep our discovery secret."

"For the moment," adds Sir Robert.

First questionings

Hampton Court
27 April 1536

In a room at Hampton Court Palace, seated next to Sir Nicholas at a table, Sir Robert prepared to question the people who had been in the Queen's rooms on the night of the murder. He was dressed in a black surplice for the occasion, with a cap of the same colour, and had adopted a solemn air. Taking from his waistcoat a folded sheet of paper, which he then spread out on the table, he proceeded to read out a list of names: Lady Margaret Lee, Lady Alice Winter, Lady Jane Rochford, Sir Henry Norris, Sir Francis Weston, Sir William Brereton, Sir George Boleyn, Sir Thomas Wyatt, Mistress Elizabeth Holland… "Almost all of noble family, it would seem, and all close to the Queen," he sighed. "Yet it is likely that one of them is the killer. Also because I have had it confirmed that neither the King nor any of his gentlemen took part in the entertainment, that the household servants slept well away from the Queen's rooms and that at that hour the gates of Whitehall would have been bolted."

"Until what hour?" asked Lady Constance.

"Until dawn, when the carts carrying fruit and vegetables from the countryside start arriving." A sigh: "So, you see, our task, besides being difficult is also a delicate one. On the other hand, as our Margery would say, one cannot make omelettes without breaking eggs."

"How do you intend to proceed?" asked Sir Nicholas.

"Simple questions. Intuition. Silence."

"Silence?"

"You see: often someone who is guilty almost feels the need to be discovered. Remorse? Over-confidence? I don't know. But when they speak, they say more than they intend to, try to find out how far we have got, and they give themselves away. So our business becomes one of knowing how to listen."

Sir Robert gestured to Philip, who was sitting beside him, and to Lady Constance and Margery, who had drawn apart into a corner of the room, preparing to work on their embroidery. "Philip will note down the salient parts of the conversation. My wife and Margery will pretend to be absorbed in their sewing, but will be all ears." He added: "Women notice the fine nuances that tend to escape us men, and often get to the heart of the matter first."

"Very true!" declared Margery approvingly.

Sir Robert sighed again. "Well then. Let us begin with the first on the list, Lady Margaret Lee. Nicholas, tell me about her."

"She is the Queen's closest friend, almost like a sister. Her brother is Sir Thomas Wyatt, the poet. The lands of the Wyatts border those of the Boleyns, their friendship dates from when they were children."

A treasure hunt

Hampton Court
27 April 1536

Lady Margaret came in to the room. She looked about thirty-five, the same age as the Queen, but she was taller, with a fuller figure, a sharp nose and thin lips set in an austere face, intelligent if not beautiful, with light wrinkles just beginning to show at the corners of her eyes. She was wearing a dark-brown dress of sumptuous velvet, edged at the collar and wrists with Bruges lace, and a single piece of jewellery, a pendant with a gold rose. Sir Robert and Sir Nicholas rose to their feet and made slight bows. Philip invited her to sit on the high-backed chair which had been placed in front of the table.

"Gentlemen," she said with a slight nod of the head and an air of aristocratic detachment. Sir Robert observed her for some moments. Then with pronounced courtesy he addressed her: "My Lady, as official investigator appointed by the sovereign, I am obliged to request that you furnish me with all the information that you can regarding the evening in which William Crooks was murdered."

She brought her hands together on her lap, then spoke in a well-mannered tone and with apparent calm. "As happens often after dinner in the Queen's rooms, we had prepared ourselves for a game. During the day objects had been hidden in different places in that wing of the Palace, and we had to find them and bring them back."

"Who was there with you?"

"Among the ladies, Lady Alice Winter, a young maid of honour to the Queen, and Lady Jane Rochford, the Queen's sister-in-law, wife of George Boleyn; Elizabeth Holland was there too. Among the gentlemen, my brother Sir Thomas Wyatt, and Sir George Boleyn, the Queen's brother. And Norris, Weston and Brereton, three gentlemen of the court. Then Master Crooks, the Queen's factotum, and the young Mark Smeaton, personal musician to the Queen."

"What did you do then?"

"Having got our instructions, we left to hunt for the treasure, each in a different direction."

"Did you all leave the room?"

"Norris, Weston and Brereton stayed behind to keep the Queen company."

'So the number of suspects falls to seven,' thought Sir Robert, and read in Sir Nicholas' eyes a confirmation of his reasoning. Unless Crooks was really blackmailing the Queen and her three friends decided to kill him. But then how to get the body to the room where it was discovered and set the scene there?'

"Would you be able to tell me what objects each of you had been sent to find?" asked Sir Robert.

"The Queen had read the list aloud to us herself."

The lady counted on her fingers: "Lady Alice had to fetch a candle; Lady Jane a shawl of embroidered blue silk; Mistress Holland a pair of blue slippers; my brother a book – a Book of Hours, I think; Sir George a silver stiletto; Smeaton a kitchen fork."

"And Crooks?"

"He did not take part in the game and had left before us."

"Why?"

"I couldn't say."

"And you, what did you have to fetch?"

"Something from the kitchen below, a bowl, the sort used for mixing spices. I was told it would be one with the red dragon of Wales embossed on the side."

"Did you find it?"

"Mistress Litcot, who is in charge of the royal kitchens, gave it to me."

"Did you speak to each other?"

"I thanked her and came away."

At that moment the midday sun flooded through the stained-glass windows, filling the room with a brilliant fretwork of colours: reds, yellows and blues.

"What happened next?"

"One after another we returned with our various objects. There was time for a game of charades, and then we went to bed."

"I was summoned not long afterwards," interposed Sir Nicholas, "because two of the ladies were unable to get into their room. It was the room where the murder took place and it had been locked from the inside."

When Lady Lee had left, Lady Constance came up to the table. "Will you go back into that room?" she asked.

"We must," replied Sir Robert. "I have to. There is a clue there, I am sure, something that I have missed, an important detail that I should remember: I try to bring it to mind, but don't manage to."

"Perhaps it is something to do with the trunks. What was there in the false bottom?"

They had not checked, and again Sir Robert felt a little foolish, as often happened with his wife. "I had thought to empty them out, but there wasn't time," he lied. "It will be our first task tomorrow."

Lady Constance smiled at him, as one does with a small child who is not telling the truth. He sought to change the subject: "Tell me, what do you make of Lady Margaret?"

"She has strong hands, but I cannot see her following Crooks with a candlestick and then slaughtering him in that fashion."

"Why not? She is tall enough," observed Sir Nicholas. He turned to Margery: "Did you notice anything?"

"She seemed to me to be anxious about something: it was clear from the way she kept on twisting her fingers together when she was talking about her brother. And she went suddenly rigid when you mentioned Elizabeth Holland."

"Who would that be?" Lady Constance asked her.

"I found out from a cook that the lady, Elizabeth Holland known as Bessie, a beautiful woman, but a commoner. She was in the service of Lady Elizabeth Stafford, the second wife of the Duke of Norfolk, she was in charge of the Lady Stafford's wardrobe and became the Duke's mistress. When Lady Stafford complained about it to her husband and called her 'his washerwoman', the Duke took offence and proceeded to beat her in front of the servants to the extent of making her spit blood."

"Bessie Holland, then. Is she a washerwoman here at court too?"

"Oh no, Lady Stafford left her husband; Bessie stayed behind with him, and he imposed her as lady-in-waiting on his niece, Anne Boleyn."

But after Lady Margaret had left the room, Sir Robert murmured, ruffling his hair with his fingers: "She appeared to be perfectly at ease, but there was a touch of embarrassment when she was speaking, as if she wished to protect someone."

Margery investigates

Hampton Court
27 April 1536

Some hours later, while they were all together to discuss the events of the morning, Margery alluded to something regarding Lady Margaret. Lady Constance and the others encouraged her to speak. She turned to Sir Robert: "Do you recall? You were uneasy, you were concerned that Lady Margaret might not have told you the whole truth."

"That's right."

"So I decided to go down to the kitchens – there I have made a friend, Nan Litcot, the head pastry cook. To uncover more facts, not to gossip, believe me."

"Of course not!" exclaimed Sir Robert.

"Well, she had just removed various cakes from the oven, and asked my opinion. We tried them together, I made some comments and lavished her with praise. Between one tasting and the next I brought the conversation about Crooks' murder and the people at court. I said: 'But what connection could there be between that Crooks and, so I've heard, a fine lady like Lady Margaret?'"

"And Nan?"

"Her? 'Oh, if you only knew!' And I: 'Please, don't tell me anything if you don't want to.''

"Which is just the way to get somebody to talk," intruded Lady Constance.

"And she wanted to, how she wanted to! 'Keep it to yourself, of course,' she said. 'Certainly', I assured her. Well: that fine lady had been in love with Mark Smeaton!"

"The queen's musician?" asked Lady Constance. "That handsome young man who writes love songs?"

"Yes, him. Many years before Mark had been one of those young men who seek their fortune at court, she had been a maid of honour to Queen Catherine. Crooks had seen them together, begun to make insinuations, to start rumours. Then to threaten, in the end to try and blackmail her."

The information would have been promising, but Sir Robert shook his head: "Look, Margery: I have checked Lady Margaret's movements that night. It is true that she went to Mistress Litcot to fetch the bowl. Yes. But it is also true that she returned immediately to the queen's rooms accompanied by the same servant who had taken her to the kitchens."

"Nan didn't tell me this."

"Why not, I wonder?"

"Simple: I didn't persist, I said goodbye and left."

"Why didn't you stay a while longer?"

"Well, perhaps I was a little tired. Or perhaps because we had finished the tasting…"

Laughter from everyone brought the conversation to a close.

A poisoned goblet

Hampton Court
27 April 1536

Towards mid-morning a servant had brought in a tray on which were a jug of cool beer and some finely engraved silver goblets. One of these, which had already been filled, he had placed directly in front of Sir Robert. All gladly availed themselves of the King's excellent beer, except Sir Robert, who took a mouthful but immediately spat it out, its taste acrid and unpleasant. 'A stupid mistake' he thought, but then began to feel his mouth burn and he started to retch.

Sir Nicholas grabbed the cup, sniffed it. "Hellebore," he pronounced, "poison!" and hurled the contents on the floor. "Constance, get him to vomit." He hurried out of the room: the young servant was disappearing down the corridor. He caught up with him, seized him by the shoulders, and spun him round. "Where does the beer that you brought us come from?"

"From the royal cellars, sir. By order of Doctor Barefoot. A treat for the guests, he said."

"The beer, did you draw it?"

"Yes, sir."

Sir Nicholas jerked him roughly. "I want the truth."

"I didn't do anything."

"Would you swear to that in front of Norfolk's guards?"

At that name the boy went pale. He stammered: "The last goblet, the very fancy one, he was holding himself. He dropped a grain of something into it, medicine perhaps. He ordered me to place it in front of Sir Robert, the doctor, and not to make a mistake."

"And he gave you…"

"A silver coin, sir."

Sir Nicholas came back into the room. "Barefoot," he announced, "it was him. But even if you had drunk the whole cupful, the amount of poison it contained would not have killed you, though you would have had a badly upset stomach."

Sir Robert was already feeling better. "It was just out of spite," he asserted, "he wanted to make a point."

"What makes you say that?"

"I have learnt that he uses some of what he earns at court to help the people from his village. He used to be very poor, and at London he has made something of himself. So there is good in him."

Lady Constance, her face pale and anxious, wiped his forehead: "Good? What good?! That creature is dangerous, he needs to be stopped. Sir Nicholas, I entreat you to report this matter to the Court doctor."

"I shall do better than that, I shall take it to the Duke of Norfolk. He'll know what to do."

A trip on the Thames

From Hampton Court to Staines
27 April 1536

Sir Robert stayed several hours in his room. He soothed his mouth with lemon balm and herbal infusions – camomile and fennel – promptly prepared by Margery, and re-read the notes that his assistant had made. In the early afternoon the Duke of Norfolk organized a fishing trip on the Thames in honour of the guests. The sky was clear, the sun bright upon the water, with the occasional gust of wind, the cries of the boatmen ferrying people from one side of the river to the other, and many brightly-coloured river craft making way for the Duke's impressive barge.

From Hampton Court the party travelled up the river to old Sudbury, and then further on, towards Walton Bridge, and further still to the neighbourhood of Saxon Weybridge, and Chertsey, and the Roman town of Staines, where a local landowner had organized lavish refreshments in the main courtyard of his house.

Taking part in the excursion, besides Sir Nicholas' guests, there were some gentlemen and two of the ladies-in-waiting to the Queen who had participated in the treasure hunt on the night of the murder – Lady Alice Winter and Bessie Holland, the Duke's mistress. When Alice seemed to hesitate in crossing the plank that led to the Duke's barge, Bessie took her hand, guided her to the prow and saw that she was comfortably seated in the shade of the canopy. Having done this, she went and sat down next to Lady Constance: the two women had taken an immediate liking to each other. Bessie had learned that Lady Constance came from a family of gentlefolk, and the governess Margery had confirmed this to her. 'Lady Constance' Bessie had thought 'is genuine, she speaks in a straightforward way and doesn't look down on me as the others do.'

"Mistress Holland," Lady Constance asked, "tell me who that young lady is that you were with a moment ago."

"Alice? Lady Alice Winter of Broughton Astley in Leicestershire. She's an orphan, and not yet twenty. She lost her parents in terrible circumstances. Now she is a maid of honour to the Queen, and also her ward." Bessie enjoyed chatting, and Lady Constance had that rare gift of knowing how to listen. "She's from a well-to-do family, knows French and can play the lute. The Queen has charged me with looking after her. We share a room. I am fond of her."

Lady Constance wondered why Bessie should be given care of the girl. After all, the two were so different: Lady Alice tall, slender, with delicate features, blond hair, long and soft, eyes dark blue like the sky on certain summer days, and with a distant expression; the other was full-figured, with a slightly upturned nose, a rich mass of red hair and a contagious laugh: one who knew what she wanted. And, in addition, was unashamedly good-looking.

While Lady Constance and Bessie were chatting, Philip had gone and sat down next to Lady Alice. He seemed to have become rather shy; she, on the other hand, her hands in her lap and her body erect, wore an inscrutable smile on her lips. For the rest of the trip the young man stayed at her side. The party arrived back at Hampton Court in the late afternoon, and when they came off the Duke's barge, he gave her his arm.

As the sun was setting, some of the Palace attendants threw food to the swans, those snow-white birds that belonged by right to the King. That evening, if Sir Robert and his people had met for their usual get-together, the young Philip would have had many things to say about the girl. But it was late and no meeting took place. It was the following day when there happened the incident with Lady Alice.

Lady Alice

Hampton Court
28 April 1536

Somewhat unsettled, Margaret Ackworth came into the room where the inquest would continue later that morning, her long grey gown brushing the floor. Breathing rather heavily, she sat down next to Lady Constance. "This place is full of ghosts," she declared.
"Have you met any on the way here?" asked Sir Robert.
"Oh, don't make fun of me. A place like this is enough to make you shudder."
Sir Nicholas came up close to her: "Mistress Ackworth, perhaps they have already told you about Herne the Hunter?"
"They have, and they said that he was seen last night wandering around the park. His dogs were yelping and he was crying."
"Whoever is this Herne?" asked Lady Constance.
"He was a young favourite of the king's, at Hampton Court his ghost has become legendary," explained Sir Nicholas. "Out of envy some courtiers began to slander him, and he lost the king's favour. So he

hanged himself on an oak tree, not far from here, in the park. And now his spirit roams around during the night, astride his hunter and surrounded by his hunting dogs."

"Just as you say, Sir Nicholas," agreed Margery.

"When one dies young," murmured Lady Constance, "one is robbed of so much of life. I can understand that one might feel a sense of nostalgia for familiar places."

At that moment, before anyone could reply, Lady Alice Winter entered the room, together with Bessie Holland. Philip went up to her and guided her to a seat in front of the table. Sir Robert, seated opposite her, seemed annoyed that the young woman was accompanied. "I had made it known that I would be interviewing one person at a time. Why are you here together?" he asked.

Philip tried to draw his attention to Lady Alice's eyes, but Sir Robert did not respond. It was the young woman herself who resolved the situation. "Thank you, Bessie. I can manage by myself now."

Bessie hugged her and left the room. Alice turned her face towards Sir Robert, who remained perplexed. Sir Nicholas intervened, with a rare degree of courtesy: "My Lady, Sir Robert is not aware of your condition."

It was then that Sir Robert noticed that there was something unusual about the woman's eyes.

"Excuse me. I don't really understand… Please explain to me, if you can," he said.

There followed a long pause, as if the young woman found it difficult to speak. Eventually, in a quiet voice: "My father was lord of a manor and owned a great deal of land in Leicestershire," she said finally. "I was the only child. My mother had taught me to sew and embroider, and all that was necessary for a woman to know to manage a house and servants. She herself kept busy providing for the needs of widows and orphans, sewing clothes for the poor, making bed sheets for expectant mothers and tending to the sick. My father had engaged for me a tutor, who taught me French, as well as reading and writing. He himself took care of the land and the administration of justice. The villagers were fond of us, and when we rode by the men would raise their hats and the women would offer us bunches of wild flowers." She sighed: "It was a good life."

She started to speak again, her voice was calm. "On the day of my sixteenth birthday we went out hunting. A storm broke, unexpected, violent. My parents happened to be next to a large oak tree, which was hit by lightning. I was a few steps behind them, with the beaters. When I reached the spot where my parents had been, they were no longer there, all that remained were their skeletons, of the horses too. Charred remnants, in the midst of fire, smoke and the smell of burning flesh…"

Lady Alice clasped her head in her hands, her voice broke, she was unable to continue. She was reliving those agonizing moments, the terrifying flash and hiss of lightning, the crackle of the flames, the sight of bones stripped bare, the stench of bodies burning, her own desperate cries. And then, suddenly, darkness.

A delicate young lady

Hampton Court
28 April 1536

It was Sir Nicholas who spoke for her.

"Burned alive," he said. "It was in that moment that everything went black around her."

"And with the passing of time?" asked Sir Robert.

"Her condition didn't improve. In an instant she could no longer see, all of a sudden she had become blind. An uncle brought her to court, where the matter was discussed, but no-one could get to the root cause of her condition: perhaps it was the blinding flash of the lightning, the crash of the thunder, the horror, the heartbreak. No-one could make sense of it."

All kept silent, moved. But Sir Robert's scientific curiosity got the better of his discomfort. "How did they try to treat her?" he asked.

"In the beginning they proposed a variety of remedies: a decoction of fennel, compresses of *angelica*, bleeding, fasting. Then exorcism was tried. Eventually, the King entrusted her to the care of the Queen, who is fond of her."

"It is easy to be so," blurted out Philip. While the others turned to look at him, she murmured: "You are kind." Going red, he went to sit at the table, where he began turning a goose quill round in his fingers, suddenly grown clumsy.

Sir Robert examined the girl's turquoise-coloured eyes. "I had not noticed, I had not realized. Please forgive me, madam," he said. Then added with sudden kindness: "You have lovely eyes."

"It's true," agreed Lady Constance. She approached the young woman and touched her gently on the shoulders. "I am Sir Robert Kytchyn's wife. Be assured that we are all friends here."

"I know," she replied with a smile of hopeless resignation. She made an effort: "And if you wish to interrogate me, I am ready."

It was the first time that Sir Robert had had to press questions on someone blind, and he was hesitant about how to begin. He imagined to himself the darkness which surrounded her and how she must feel amongst strangers whose expressions she could not see. How could he persuade her of his sympathetic attitude? In an almost timid voice he began by asking her if she had been present at the party in the Queen's rooms on the evening of the twenty-fourth of April. Lady Alice nodded: "And after dinner, the Queen had proposed a game in which each of us had to hunt for and bring back a particular object."

"You, what did you have to fetch?"

"A candle."

"Did Mistress Holland go with you?"

"No."

"But how could you have…?"

"It wasn't difficult. Our rooms are not very far from those of the Queen. I would take a candle from one of the candlesticks in the hall."

"Did you find one?"

"No. And I came back empty-handed."

"Do you remember what happened after that?"

"Sooner or later we all came back, each with their particular objects. There was time for a game of charades, and eventually we all went to bed."

Sir Robert thanked her and Philip went to call Mistress Holland, who came to accompany her out.

"The rest we know: the door locked from the inside, etcetera. I would say that we can remove her from the list," declared Sir Robert. "We know that a crime requires a motive, together with both the means and the opportunity. Now, what could there have been between her and that scoundrel? What motive? And as for means: how could a delicate girl, above all one who is blind…?"

Sir Nicholas agreed with him: "In these last few days I have had occasion to observe that young woman. I am sure that, given her condition, she could never aim at someone's head and face with such accuracy. All of which leads us to the conclusion that someone else is responsible."

Margery's eyes shone with mischief. "With due respect: but have you noticed how men always have a

76

weakness for pretty vulnerable women?" she murmured in Lady Constance's ear. The latter looked at her husband, as if about to say something to him, then gave a slight smile and chose to remain silent.

'Ring-a-ring-of-roses.'

Hampton Court,
28 April 1536

The afternoon was warm and fine. In the gardens
adjacent to the courtyard of the fountain, some
children, from among the families of palace workers,
were playing ring-a-ring-o'-roses, holding hands and
running round in a circle. The words of the rhyme
could be clearly heard:
'Ring-a-ring o' roses,
A pocketful of posies,
Atishoo, atishoo,
We all fall down.'

With the prospect of such a pleasant day, Sir Robert
had decided to continue with the interviews in the
open air, on the terrace to the east of the house, facing
the park. Margery had protested at the idea. "Actually
here, where that poor boy hanged himself. You are
very insensitive, I shall die of fright." However,
despite her complaints, she had decided that she must
stay at Lady Constance's side.

Meanwhile they had been joined on the terrace by Sir Thomas Wyatt, the poet, brother of Lady Margaret: a handsome man around thirty, tall and well built, with light-grey eyes and a crop of red hair visible under his cap. A beard, bristly and long, covered his cheeks and chin. A childhood friend of Anne Boleyn, he had fallen in love with her when, at the age of twenty, she had returned to England from France and by then was a woman, elegant and confident. But his had been a hopeless love because when King Henry had begun to court her, he had had to draw away.

Sir Robert had presented his wife to him: "Sir Thomas, Lady Constance is enchanted by your sonnets."

That man, tall and imposing as he was, had reddened like a boy. "I am honoured," he had replied with a bow.

He sat down.

"Now I must ask you about your movements on the night of the crime," said Sir Robert.

"I… I was there."

"Excuse me, where exactly?"

"At dinner. Then in the treasure hunt. And then I took part in the charades."

"Where did you have to search for your treasure?"

"In my rooms, in the guests' wing."

"I have a map of Whitehall. Can you show me that wing?"

Sir Thomas came over to the table and pointed with his finger. "Here, next to the private rooms."

"It is reached via the corridor?"

"I had decided to go through the courtyard instead, I wanted to look at the stars."

"Did you see them?"

"Yes. The bright April stars."

Sir Robert sat down again, brought the tips of his fingers together, rested his chin on them and half closed his eyes in the manner of the cat which has the mouse under its paws: "I have been informed that it was raining that night."

Sir Thomas seemed taken aback. "Perhaps I was wrong."

"Perhaps." A pause. "Did you find what you were looking for?"

"And I brought it back."

"What was it?"

"A manuscript, a translation of Seneca that I had just finished."

"Not a Book of Hours, as your sister says?"

Again Wyatt seemed uneasy. "It may have been. I don't really remember."

"They tell me that when the murder was discovered, you were distraught."

"These bloody days have broken my heart..."

"Did you hear any unusual sounds, did you see anyone running away?"

Sir Robert waited a long while for a reply that did not come: the man seemed uneasy and eventually, when he was told that he could go, he left in a hurry, almost stumbling on the paving stones.

After Sir Thomas had left, they all looked at each other puzzled. "The height would be right, and the physical strength is there. And he was certainly lying when he talked of the stars and the book," said Sir Robert.

"He and his sister might bring themselves to kill for the Queen. If there was a question of blackmail on Crook's part, anything is possible," added Sir Nicholas.

"Sir Robert, you said that it would be Crooks himself who led us to the murderer," murmured Philip.

"What are you all muttering about?" exclaimed Lady Constance. "Of course he was confused. His world is so different from ours. Didn't you hear how sad he sounded, how his heart bled when he talked of these troubled times?"

Margery added: "And then, he is so handsome. With killers, you can always see in their faces that they are wicked."

"Not always, Margery, not always," murmured Sir Robert.

Sir Thomas' Night

Hampton Court
28 April 1536

"Not always, Margery, not always," repeated Sir Robert. "And not in order to prove you wrong, but I have made searching enquiries about him. Nicholas, I have interrogated the gentleman of the bedchamber of Sir Thomas. Do you know him?"

"Of course: a prudent, discreet man. He won't have opened his mouth to anyone, I imagine."

"And very reserved. So much so that it needed a rather large sum on my part to loosen his tongue. In the end, these were his words: 'That evening Sir Thomas entered his chamber to fetch the object. He seated himself at the table: 'I'm writing a note for someone, then I shall return to the celebration. Wait outside for me, I'll tell you who to take it to.' But then…

'Then what?'

'He didn't come out again. I waited for him, seated on a chest in the entrance hall. After a good while, perhaps a couple of hours, I knocked at the door. There was no reply. I was worried. I went in. He was still there, bent over the desk, pen in hand as if writing. And he was asleep.'

'And you?'

'I was tired too. So I took a large tome from the bookshelf and dropped it on the floor. He woke with a start. On the desk the candle had almost burnt down to the midnight notch. 'It's grown late,' he said, 'the banquet will be over by now.' So I helped him prepare for the night, as I always do.'

'Are you sure that he didn't leave the room again?'

'Absolutely certain – that night too it was my turn to sleep on the straw mattress outside his door.''

"The tapestry slowly moved…"

Hampton Court
28 April 1536

Later it was the turn of Bessie Holland, who proved talkative and showy, in a very low-cut dress. It was a brief interview, because the slippers that she was to fetch in the hunt were those of Jane Rochford: Lady Jane herself had let her into her room, with the result that the two women had undertaken the search together and would be witness for one another. No, they had seen nothing, and heard nothing, and had been the first to return to the Queen's room.

"Mistress Holland," said Sir Robert, "Lady Rochford is the wife of Sir George Boleyn, Viscount Rochford, is that right?"

"Indeed it is!"

"Meaning?"

"To put an end to talk regarding a rumoured relationship with the Queen's musician – there was a lot of gossip about it at court – Sir George was obliged to marry that woman, ugly and vindictive."

"Poor man…"

"But the pair hate each other: she is jealous, he keeps well away from her. You will have met her at Hampton Court, I imagine."

'I was seated next to her at table, the first time at Hampton Court' Sir Robert thought to himself. 'I posed certain questions to her, briefly and delicately, in view of her rank, and she recalled having heard and seen nothing. As for Bessie Holland' he reflected, 'she is a pleasant woman, but one gets nowhere interrogating her. Unless…' He frowned. "Tell me: the room that you share with Lady Alice is the one in which Crooks was killed?"

"Unfortunately so, and that night they had to move us elsewhere."

"Have you been back?

"Not even to collect our things."

"On the wall in front of the bed there is a tapestry?"

"More an old dusty rag than a tapestry."

"Have you ever moved it, perhaps to have it cleaned?"

The woman hesitated. She looked around as if seeking a means of escape. She sought Lady Constance's eyes: a look passed between the two women, Constance gave her a slight nod. "Well, Lady Alice told me that for some time there had been something at night-time which had disturbed her: like a presence."

"A ghost?" whispered Margery.

"Certainly not a ghost. I sleep soundly, I had never noticed anything, but one evening Alice begged me to stay awake with her. She clung to me, she knows that I am fond of her. We left a candle alight, and I told her to pinch me if I fell asleep. At a certain moment we

85

heard a noise, but we were not sure where it came from."

The woman's cheeks were glowing, her lips curled as if she had tasted something unpleasant: "Very slowly the tapestry moved. And who did we find next to our bed? That animal, Crooks!"

"Mistress Holland, do you remember when it was that you found Crooks in the room?"

"Sometime before the treasure hunt, towards dawn. From that moment I tried never to leave Alice Alone, as far as was possible. But he pursued her."

"How do you mean?"

"He wanted her to become his lover. When she refused he began to spread malicious lies about us two, and then threatened us with blackmail."

When Mistress Holland had left, Sir Robert shared his recent thoughts: "That woman is taller than Crooks – she's strong, decisive. And he was threatening her too,"

He sighed, raised his spectacles, passed a hand through his hair. He concluded: "And that night she could have killed him."

Philip looked at him in dismay: "The same could be said of Lady Alice, in the room with her! She might have been an accomplice..."

A bundle of letters

London, Whitehall Palace
1 May 1536, May Day

Something had troubled Sir Robert all night. On
waking he remembered nothing of his dreams but,
although it was a feast day – that morning the court
would be moving to Greenwich for the May Day
celebrations, tournaments and fancy dress, banquets
and dancing – he decided instead to return with his
companions to Whitehall, to the scene of the crime,
and asked Sir Nicholas and Philip to accompany him.

The room of the murder was as they had left it, except
that the candlestick had been removed and the blood
cleaned from the floor. There was dust in the air and
little flecks of light danced in the shaft of sunlight
which streamed in through the gap between the
shutters.

They threw open the windows, and with relief
breathed the fresh air. Sir Nicholas and Philip raised
the heavy lid of the first chest, the one nearest the
door, and took out dresses, surcoats, shawls and a red,
fur-lined cloak, head-dresses, all rather gaudy, and

some misshapen silk shoes. In the false bottom were some jewels, of little value.

"These must belong to Mistress Holland," observed Sir Nicholas.

They opened the other chest. Here too were gowns, tunics, stockings, a pair of high-quality leather shoes, and a leaf-green cloak which they laid out on the bed. This was tasteful clothing. Some precious jewels in a small casket and, wrapped in a soft blue cloth, a manuscript illuminated in gold and blue: the ballads of Guillaume de Machaut.

"A memento of when Lady Alice could read," murmured Philip, holding it between his hands.

"Nothing in the false bottom," said Sir Nicholas, "But here there is a bundle of letters."

After they had replaced everything in the chests, he handed the bundle of letters to Sir Robert, who untied the string which bound them. He chose one. It was signed 'Your ever faithful William'."

"William Crooks, perhaps?" remarked Sir Robert. "I should feel uncomfortable reading these without Lady Alice's consent. But if this William is William Crooks, and there was some link between the two of them, then we have a duty to discover it."

On hearing that name Philip felt a sudden pang in his stomach: 'Jealousy? A silly idea,' he said to himself. Nevertheless he turned to Sir Robert: "With your permission, sir, I could take them to her and read them with her." He looked at Sir Robert as a young dog looks at his master. He hesitated. "She herself could explain."

"But if there was something behind it, you would not hide it from me, would you?"

"What makes you think that?"

Sir Robert put a hand on his shoulder, his eyes smiling: "The fact that you are falling in love with her, my boy. You are the only one that doesn't realize it."

Later, seated on the edge of the bed, Sir Robert reflected: "We must go into that tunnel again, see if we have missed something, a recess, a mark on the wall, any sort of clue," he said finally.

Sir Nicholas went out of the room and returned with a lantern. Then he and Philip moved aside the tapestry and entered the narrow passage. Sir Robert followed them. They went ahead very slowly, scrutinizing the ground, the walls and the roof: nothing, apart from spiders' webs and beetles, which scurried away into cracks in the walls. They arrived at the kitchens.

"Shall we go in?" asked Sir Nicholas. They all agreed. They filed in through the half-open door. There were few people at work at that time of the day, a cook who stood beside a large fireplace with her back to them, and two scullery boys seated on stools, busy plucking some chickens.

Sir Nicholas greeted the woman with a playful bow: "Mistress Litcot, a happy May Day to you."

Though rather surprised, the woman curtsied in return: "Sir Nicholas, a happy day to you. And to you gentlemen," she added on seeing Sir Robert and Philip.

Sir Nicholas sat down on a bench by a table and motioned to his friends to do likewise. "My dear lady, I have spoken to these gentlemen of your wonderful ginger cakes. You wouldn't happen…"

The woman beamed with pleasure. "For you, Sir Nicholas, always!" And she served them cake and whipped cream, followed by marzipan and beer.

"Mistress Litcot," said Sir Nicholas after they had devoured a large quantity of sweets under the contented gaze of the woman, "this gentleman is Sir Robert Kytchyn, a doctor who studies crimes. The King has charged him with investigating the case you know, of William Crooks."

"May he rest in peace," she said, crossing herself several times.

"Indeed. Now tell me: that evening of the Queen's last party before the court moved to Hampton Court, do you recall if anyone came to fetch anything?"

"Yes, Lady Margaret. She was looking for a bowl with the red dragon of Wales. I handed it to her myself."

"Do you remember which door she came in through?" The woman looked at him with a puzzled expression. "There is only one door, the one which opens into the hallway."

"Not by that small door?" and Sir Robert indicated the one at the end of the tunnel.

"That one? No, it's always locked, only Crooks had the key. Who knows who has it now, perhaps his friend Master Barefoot."

"How do the dishes get to the banqueting hall?"

"We use those hoists at the end."

She showed them to him. He put his head into the tunnel: the walls were smooth and whitewashed. From above shone down the light from the banqueting hall.

"And do you remember Smeaton?"

"Smeaton…"

"The queen's musician."

"No, that evening I didn't see him."

"And if he had come?"

"I should have certainly noticed him."

In the Queen's rooms

London, Palace of Whitehall
May Day, 1536

"Smeaton had to fetch a kitchen fork, a skewer, something of that kind," Sir Robert said later. Another mystery. Why didn't he come to the kitchen? We must question him, check his times."

"He too is in love with the Queen," explained Sir Nicholas. "Certainly he would have done anything for her if he had thought her to be in danger."

"Could he have followed Crooks into the secret passage, and then killed him?" Sir Robert speculated.

"He's young and only slightly built. He could never have managed that with a brute like Crooks."

"If he had had to fight him, no. But if he had taken him by surprise?"

"And why is it that Mistress Litcot, who has eyes everywhere, did not notice him that evening?"

"Before questioning him, I suggest that we have a look at the Queen's room, to see if there is some connection between the two," said Sir Robert.

"For example?"

"Some dedication on a sheet of music, anything written…"

They made their way there. From the corridor which ran the length of the royal rooms, at present deserted, one entered a small antechamber containing two chests and some stools. Out of this a heavy door opened into a rather large room, panelled in beech, with three high windows. Off the end was Anne Boleyn's private room.

This was as the Queen had left it some days before, the morning of 24 April, when the court had moved to Hampton Court: the air was still scented with the lavender from her clothes. On a bench beside her unmade bed there lay a variety of objects. Sir Nicholas picked up a sky-blue shawl with long fringes. There was also a pair of elegant blue slippers; a book with the monogram of Sir Thomas Wyatt on the cover, a costly Florentine stiletto, a wooden spice bowl.

"There's no trace of Smeaton's fork," said Sir Robert.

Just at that moment they heard the door of the room open and the sound of footsteps. They looked at each other and without speaking drew back into the shadow, against the wall.

There entered two young men: one dark-haired, rather emaciated and with a restless air, the other some years older, blond, sturdy. Both handsome and elegantly dressed in velvet, they spoke in a low voice and held hands.

Sir Nicholas emerged from the shadow and made a slight bow: "Sir George," he said.

George Boleyn pulled his hand away from that of his friend. "Sir Nicholas."

"Sir George, allow me to present Sir Robert Kytchyn, whom the king has entrusted with investigating the death of William Crooks."

Sir George and his friend exchanged glances. Embarrassment? Fear?

"And Master Philip Glover is Sir Robert's assistant."

In his turn George Boleyn presented his companion: "Mark Smeaton, the Queen's musician. We have come here to Whitehall from Hampton Court to retrieve an object," he declared. In a relaxed manner he approached the bench, picked up the stiletto by its silver hilt, slipped it in his belt, put his hand on Smeaton's shoulder: "Gentlemen…" he said, and made as if to leave with a brief salutation.

"To tell the truth, Sir George, I was anxious to having the honour of meeting you," explained Sir Robert respectfully, planting himself in front of the door. The other nodded.

"While Sir Nicholas exchanges a few words with Master Smeaton, I would like to ask you some questions. If you don't mind," he added.

They sat down, while Sir Nicholas led Smeaton into another room.

Smeaton, uncertain, cast a glance at George Boleyn, who in turn replied: "It's all right, Mark."

"What did you have to fetch for the Queen on the night of the treasure hunt?" Sir Nicholas asked Mark Smeaton.

"A kitchen fork. That's to say, a short skewer. The sort that chickens are roasted on."

"And how is it that we have not seen it in the other room?"

"Because I never got to the kitchen. I met Sir George and went with him to his rooms to look for the dagger. It was getting late and we went back to the Queen."

"Did you bear a grudge of any kind against Crooks?"

"I detested him, as did everyone: he was too powerful, he held the Queen in his grasp, with the help of that slimy Barefoot. But if you think that I killed him, you are mistaken. I was with Sir George, as he will tell you."

George Boleyn confirmed Smeaton's testimony word for word, almost as if the two had agreed on this together.

Later, having returned to Lady Alice's room. Sir Nicholas gave orders that the two chests be locked, secured with leather belts and loaded on the barge to be taken to Hampton Court. "The ladies will be pleased to have their belongings back," he said.

When they went back aboard the boat for the return to Hampton Court, Sir Robert checked that the bag into which he had slipped Crooks' letters was properly fastened. He then sat down in the prow, without speaking. Only when they were in sight of the red walls of the royal residence did he take the bundle of letters out of the bag and hand it to his assistant. "Do as you said, Philip, read them to Lady Alice."

He added: "I am willing to trust you."

The tragedy

Hampton Court
1 May 1536, May Day

The sun was setting as Sir Robert, Sir Nicholas and Philip arrived back at Hampton Court. The breeze that had been with them on the river had softened and the fields were full with the scents of approaching summer. But when Lady Constance came to meet them at the wharf, they could see that she was troubled. This was such an unusual sight that even the usually placid Sir Robert was concerned. He exchanged a few words with her, then turned to Sir Nicholas and Philip: "It is something to do with the Queen," he said, "you'd better come into my rooms."

They did so, and as a precaution went to the far end, well away from the door. Lady Constance and Sir Robert sat down in the window-seat, Sir Nicholas and Philip on a bench in front of them. Margery stayed standing, and kept making sure that there was no-one listening in the corridor outside.

Sir Robert put an arm round his wife's shoulders. "Now, tell us. What has happened?"

"I don't know how to explain, it is all so difficult to understand."

"Start at the beginning, take your time."

"Well, this morning we left the court and went down the river as far as Greenwich, where the Mayday celebrations were to be held. There were crowds of people come to admire the procession of knights: their attire, the colourful caparisons of the horses, the standards fluttering in the air, the suits of armour shining. Magnificent. The tournament began: the Queen wanted me next to her on the stand, with her ladies. On the platform nearby sat the King with his gentlemen – sulky, though, now that the wound on his leg prevents him from taking part in the way he used to."

"Who did the Queen give her colours to?"

"To her brother, Sir George Boleyn, who was to face a French knight. The tournament promised to be exciting, but after a couple of runs, the Lord Chancellor Sir Thomas Cromwell, dressed all in black like a crow, approached the King and showed him a paper. The King read it, got to his feet, went up to the queen, gave her an evil look and whispered something in her ear. Then, without another word, he left the tournament, headed towards the landing-stage and gave orders to return to Hampton Court. From our seats we could see the royal barge making its way up the river, moving to the rhythm of the drum, which beat time for the oarsmen."

The sunlight fell aslant the small leaded panes of the window, filling the room with a soft, pearly light, whilst outside the wind had risen again.

"And the Queen?" asked Sir Robert.

"Ashen-faced, trembling all over. She continued sitting a little while longer, then directed that we return to Hampton Court without remaining for the evening entertainments, while she sought refuge with one or two ladies at the palace at Greenwich. She seemed terrified.

Indifferent to these dramatic events, the sun shone obliquely on the small panes of glass in the window, filling the room with light. Outside the wind had risen again.

And Lady Constance, snuggling close to her husband: "Oh Robert, what can the King have said to her? What more is going to happen?"

Perhaps he'll send her to the stake

Hampton Court
2 May 1536

The following morning everyone at Hampton Court, the servants the first of all, came to hear about the calamitous events of the previous evening at Greenwich Palace: someone had arrived at Anne Boleyn's rooms, one of her ladies had gone to wake her: "The Lord Chancellor and the Keeper of the Tower are here, with some soldiers," she had been told. In an arrogant manner Cromwell had brushed past the lady and walked straight into the Queen's bedchamber, where she was still in her nightshirt, bare-footed beside the bed. "Lady Anne," he had declared, with a slight bow, "you are accused of high treason, adultery and incest. I have orders to escort you to the Tower, where you will be held prisoner at the king's pleasure."

He had called her 'Lady Anne', not 'Your Grace'. The queen had looked at him bewildered, without understanding; a lady had gathered together some clothes for her, and a prayer book, and had made her put on a dress and a velvet cloak. She had pulled the hood down so as to hide her face, and no further words had been spoken.

The courtiers who had arrived from Greenwich that morning reported having heard the measured step of the guards echoing in the night down the stairway and into the hall. Outside it was raining, they had said, the night was dark, without moon or stars, and when they had arrived at the landing stage, an oarsman had held the Queen's hand to help her into the barge that would take her to the fortress: she had thanked him for that gesture of respect, and he had been the only one to see her tears.

All the servants in the royal household were talking about it: "It's all because King Harry has fallen madly in love with Lady Jane and wants to marry her. That's why."

"The Seymours produce lots of children, and he is sure that she will give him an heir."

"And since it took six years to divorce good Queen Catherine, this time he is going to work quickly to rid himself of her, he's accusing Anne Boleyn of treason, and see if he doesn't have her condemned!"

"Perhaps he'll send her to the stake. I heard him shouting at her: 'You're a witch! You have cast a spell on me. That's the reason for my rotten leg!' And they burn witches, don't they?"

"But why accuse her of having so many lovers? Wouldn't one have been enough?"

"Oh no. If it had been only one, people would have said: 'Poor old Harry, he couldn't manage it any more, and she has taken a young lover.' But if there are a lot, then he is the victim and she is the whore who must be punished."

"And the five, who would they be?" Lady Constance asked Sir Nicholas.

"Sir Henry Norris, the king's closest friend: they fought together in France. A handsome man, came to court as a boy. He used to go hawking with the King, to the tournaments, kept guard sleeping on a mattress outside his door. And Sir Francis Weston, the sovereign's personal page. Sir William Brereton, one of the chamberlains. Mark Smeaton, the young court musician. And even Sir George Boleyn, the Queen's brother."

"Absurd. I have known them all, especially George – he was always teasing me when we were children." Lady Constance appeared upset. "We know that Anne was ambitious, sometimes overbearing. And the people certainly loved Queen Catherine more. But in all these years she has always been devoted to the king. More than once she has written: 'He has raised me to be queen; I owe him my gratitude.' She would never have fallen so low."

And Margery, clasping her hands together: "Dear Lord, where does the truth lie?"

"I was condemned to live…"

**Hampton Court
2 May 1536**

Philip Glover did not manage to meet Lady Alice until the following afternoon. He had explained the reason for wishing to do so to Mistress Holland, and now the three of them were sitting together in the fountain courtyard, on a stone bench, in the shade.

Philip saw that both women had been crying.

"What a tragedy, Master Glover," said Bessie. "There is no news of the Queen, and Norris, Brereton, Weston and George Boleyn have been shut in the Tower. The King is nowhere to be seen, they say that he is still with the Seymours, at Wolf Hall."

"The Queen's musician had also disappeared," murmured Lady Alice, "but today it was made known that he too is a prisoner in the Tower."

"Let me tell you about the trap that Chancellor set for him," burst out Bessie. "One evening Cromwell invited him for an evening meal. Smeaton was flattered by this: he comes from a humble background and has made his way at court solely on the strength of his music."

"Love songs that break your heart, and a sweet voice," added Lady Alice quietly, and Philip again felt the sharp stabbing pain that he had experienced the other day, at the discovery of Crooks' letters.

"Cromwell invited him," continued Bessie, "and when they had sat down at table, instead of having the dinner served, the Chancellor started to ask about the medal that the other was wearing around his neck. Smeaton boasted: 'It is a gift of Queen Anne's, sir. Solid gold!'

'And the expensive cloak that you were wearing when you arrived?'

'That too is a gift of the Queen. Florentine velvet.'

'So the Queen showers you with presents. What does she wish to thank you for?'

A threatening note in Cromwell's voice alarmed the musician. 'She likes my songs. She is generous.'

'Because you get into her bed?'

'No!'

At that moment two guards entered the room and placed themselves at Smeaton's shoulders. He denied the charge vehemently, but Cromwell had him taken to the Tower. The boy is not high-born, so they will be able to torture him. They'll make him confess all that Cromwell wants."

The woman became silent, as did Philip and Lady Alice, as if they could hear the screams of the young man suffering.

"Mistress Holland," Philip said at length, "I must now talk with Lady Alice about certain matters concerning the night of the murder. Alone. On Sir Robert's orders," he hastened to add.

Only when the woman had left did Philip realize how difficult his task was going to be. Why hadn't he left it to Sir Robert to deal with? Why did those letters scorch his doublet so?

"Lady Alice," he started.

She turned towards him, and Philip noticed that she didn't look at his eyes but at somewhere beyond his face.

"Lady Alice," he repeated. "Sir Robert has asked me…You see, we have a duty to…"

He could not bring himself to talk about the cursed letters, and changed subjects. "How do you find being at court?"

She sensed his discomfort and answered softly: "The Queen is good to me, almost like a mother. But recently she has been tormented by something: one day I overheard her talking to her chaplain about the little Elizabeth: 'If some misfortune should befall me' she was saying to him. And he 'We are in God's hands, my lady.' And again she: 'But if the worst should happen, dress her as a boy and get her away, to France, to some safe place.' And she gave him money. And now we, here, can do nothing for her, still less I."

Philip grasped her hand fervently, she did not pull it away but continued in a downcast tone: "We cannot do anything, while I would like so much to be at her side. When the King entrusted me to her, three years ago, I had lost everything."

"I can well imagine how you felt. The sudden death of your parents, then finding yourself here, almost as a servant, after you had been used to being served…"

"Oh, it is not that, but the harshness of the tragedy. Misfortunes occur, I know, we all know it. But they happen to others. When they strike us, we are not prepared. We are, as it were, unarmed."

"Lady Alice…"

"They had been taken: why they and not I? At night I kept on re-living that scene in my sleep, I kept on having nightmares about it, seeing figures without faces. And guilt. I was alive, but the life that had been granted me was a painful privilege."

"Lady Alice…"

"I was condemned to live, do you understand? While I would rather have died too."

"So she will be tried."

**Hampton Court
2 May 1536**

Philip looked at her disconsolately, examined her delicate face, her well-formed mouth, her golden hair, which reached half-way down her back; he imagined the shape of her shoulders and her young breasts under the light dress. He was almost ashamed of looking at her, since she could not be aware of his gaze. What dignity in that girl, how much courage! He would have liked to say something to her, but he feared that his voice would catch in his throat, that he would say the wrong things. He was afraid of losing her before he had told her…What? That he loved her? "I…," he stammered, then stopped.

Thus the two of them sat without speaking, hand in hand, as dusk drew nigh.

That evening, in Lady Constance's rooms, Margery reported what she had learnt from the wife of one of the Tower guards: "I had prepared an ointment of marigold and lemon-balm, for her face, and she had wanted to chat. 'So it's true that they have tortured the

Queen's musician?' I asked her. And she: "Down in the dungeons they pulled out his fingernails, burnt the soles of his feet with red-hot irons, ducked his head in and out of a pail of water and stuck a collar with iron nails inside around his neck.' 'And he?' I asked. 'In the end, to avoid being broken on the wheel, he admitted everything that they wanted him to confess: that the Queen had committed adultery with Sir Henry Norris, Sir Francis Weston, Sir William Brereton, and even with her own brother, Sir George.'"

The five looked at one another, all greatly saddened, indifferent to the jug of the King's fine wine which stood untouched on the table.

"I'm afraid that this development makes difficulties for us," said Sir Robert, passing a hand over his forehead. "Mark Smeaton would have been an important witness, as would Sir George: I should have liked to question them again. But I wonder, with what is happening, does it still make sense for us to proceed with the enquiry? In truth we were working for the Queen."

"We were working for the Duke of Norfolk, which is perhaps worse now that his enemies the Seymours seem set to become powerful," responded Sir Nicholas. "But the Duke has ordered that the investigation go ahead, he believes that our discovering the truth will be to his niece's advantage. By the way, he will be presiding over the commission that is due to try the Queen."

"So, she is to be tried," murmured Lady Constance," as if an ordinary woman."

108

Later Sir Robert asked Philip if he had managed to talk with Lady Alice. The young man hesitated, made as if to defend himself, then lowered his head, the bundle of letters still in his pocket.

"Why can't you bring yourself to do it?" the other asked.

"Short, fat, old and bleary-eyed..."

Hampton Court
3 May 1536

The following morning – it was the third of May –
Philip contrived a further meeting with Lady Alice. He
led her along the river, she leaning on his arm, and
invited her to sit down in the shade of a willow tree,
happy when she requested that he join her. "If you see
the sky darkening, please escort me back to the
palace," she asked him. 'She is terrified of storms,' he
thought, and reassured her: "Don't be afraid: it's a
calm day, the sky deep blue, the riverbank full of
flowers."
"I know. I can smell the fragrance." When she smiled,
she revealed a row of perfect teeth, small and white.
Then – and she was suddenly abrupt: "Why have you
asked to see me?" 'As if she didn't know,' thought
Philip. He took out the letters and tossed them into
her lap, he too acting brusquely.
Lady Alice started, then ran her fingers over the
bundle, and handed it back to Philip. "Crooks' letters.
You may read them, if you wish."

"I have no desire to do so. It is merely my responsibility to see that the investigation is thorough." 'Why do I wish to hurt her?' he wondered.

After a moment of silence, he took the first letter out of the bundle and read it aloud:

"My Lady, my respects and esteem. Would you please have Mistress Holland read this letter to you? I have watched you for several days and now feel moved to ask you to become the lady of my heart. It would be advantageous for you: you are alone and I have a good position at court.

Your humble servant, William Crooks."

"The lady of my heart," she repeated coldly. "What hypocritical phrasing: he means simply 'my lover'. She sighed. "You may continue."

He opened the second letter:

Madam. Why do you avoid me? Why is it, when I seek to come near you, that you have yourself led away? Is it perhaps that you hold me to be unworthy of you?

Your ever faithful William Crooks."

'So she refused him,' thought Philip, his heart warming within him.

The third letter read:

"I have the means to make you mine, whether you will or no. Be careful, madam!

Your William."

"It was all a series of growing threats," murmured Lady Alice, "until one night Bessie and I found him in our room. We started screaming, a guard knocked on our door, and Crooks fled back down the passage We pushed one of the chests against that door behind the tapestry, and another against the main door of the room. The next day we explored the secret corridor and found it led to the kitchens. We had a strong bolt nailed to the tapestry door. But I was terrified." The shadow of a smile crossed her face: "Besides, Bessie had described him to me: small, fat, old, bleary-eyed, his neck covered in pimples."

"Lady Alice…"

"And he stank: I could smell him at a distance. Then those horrible letters, and that night in the room. I am sure that he had been there before, when we were sleeping, perhaps he had touched me with those vile hands…"

Philip noticed that her eyes seemed to be filling with tears.

"Lady Alice, listen to me. Please, listen to me. He is no longer here, it is all over, there is nothing more to fear."

"He's gone, but it isn't over for me."

"Alice, I beg you," and he noticed that she had very beautiful eyes, of that intense blue which sometimes fills the summer sky. He put his arm around her shoulders, she touched his face with her hand: "You have a soft beard, and a gentle face," she whispered. "What colour are your eyes?"

"Chestnut. My hair too."

"You are young."

"Oh no, I am almost twenty!"

"Why are you here?"

"My father is dead, my mother apprenticed me to Sir Robert in order that he might make a doctor of me."

"Will you become one?"

"I would have liked to do something quite different: write poetry, compose songs. To be a musician."

A cloud of sadness passed across her face. "I too used to love music, and I still play the lute," she murmured.

That Simon Barefoot

London, Palace of Whitehall
8 May 1536

Several days passed as if suspended in unreal time: no news of the Queen, no order from London, while full summer was approaching, the villagers were working in the fields around the palace, the evenings were becoming lighter and the nights shorter, and no-one spoke about the matter of William Crooks. Sir Robert, however, continued to re-read his notes, discussed them with his wife and with Philip, wrote long detailed hypotheses. And was troubled.

On Monday the eighth of May it became known that Sir Thomas Wyatt had also been taken by night to the Tower, and therefore, in the absence of the King, the Duke of Norfolk had given orders that the court return to the capital. Meanwhile the young Philip and Lady Alice continued to meet, increasingly taken with one another, and, despite everything, immersed in their own private happiness. "Besides, one does not need a reason to be happy. One is happy or unhappy by nature, and those two are so young..." Lady

Constance had observed one day when she had seen them walking together by the river.

"But don't forget," Sir Robert had remarked to his assistant, "that even Lady Alice is among the suspects. Try not to confound personal matters with your duty."

When the court had returned to London, a new fact emerged: that Simon Barefoot, 'that so-called doctor', as Sir Nicholas called him, was discovered searching for something in the murder room. "I am assisting the investigation," he protested, "and I am astonished to see that the two chests have gone. Who took it on themselves to remove them? And why wasn't I told?"

"And why the devil should you have been consulted?" Sir Robert answered him. "Instead I would like to know how it is that you managed to gain access to the bedroom, given that it had been left locked? What relationship did you have with those two ladies? What was your relationship with William Crooks? Perhaps you both used the secret passage in order to come and spy on Mistress Holland and Lady Alice? Were you jealous of Crooks? Was it you that got rid of him?"

Sir Robert's tone was uncharacteristically menacing, the accusations serious: Barefoot looked at him in terror, threw up his arms in confusion and fled.

So Sir Robert gave orders for Barefoot to be called for further questioning. "But I don't think he is guilty, he is too timid to carry out an act which after all requires some courage. At best," he added laughing, "he might be able to tell us something about that distinctive hellebore beer."

Philip's torment

London, Palace of Whitehall
8 May 1536

On the day of the return to London, Philip managed
to speak to Lady Constance alone.

"There is something that is worrying me. I have need
of you, my lady, of your advice."

"Is it about Lady Alice?"

"How did you guess?"

"I can read it in your eyes, Philip. You may keep silent
with your lips, but your eyes speak the truth."

"So there is no need for me to explain matters to you.
I want to marry her."

"And she?"

"She loves me."

"The King's permission is required."

"We shall seek it."

"You will become rich, she has lands and properties."

"That is the last of my thoughts."

Sunlight filled the room, making Lady Constance's
flame-coloured hair gleam. Busy embroidering a shirt
for her husband: she made a final blue stitch on the

white cloth, secured it behind, laid down the work and gestured to Philip to come and sit beside her on the bench. "So, tell me."

"My lady, Sir Robert has warned me not to mix my private concerns with our enquiries, and I accept that. But every day Alice says things that make me feel so close to her, as if we had known one another elsewhere and have now found each other again. The same thoughts, the same dreams. When I am near her I seem to become entrapped by a passion for higher things."

"I know that passion, Sir Robert was possessed by it, at the beginning. It will pass, believe me."

Margery, who was entering the room, sensed that she should leave them alone, and went away.

Philip continued: "Here is what worries me. I too have examined the cards, have checked everyone's times and movements. Do you recall? Lady Margaret Lee returned to the Queen's rooms almost immediately: as a matter of fact to get there from the kitchen, she only had to go up a flight of steps and cross a corridor, and that this happened was confirmed by the three gentlemen that had stayed with the Queen. Even if she had been able to commit the crime – she is tall and strong enough, she would not have had the time. Do you agree?"

Lady Constance nodded her assent, and added: "I recollect too that the testimonies of Mistress Holland and Jane Rochford concurred, what each of them had to find was in Lady Jane's room, and for that reason

117

they went there together. I don't think either that they would have had sufficient time to carry out the crime given that they returned very promptly to the others, and the three gentlemen attest to that too."

"Unless they had planned the murder very carefully, and had committed it together: but at that point we would need to establish both means and motive," said Philip.

The young man started to pace up and down the room. "Sir Thomas Wyatt, do you still rule him out?" he asked.

"I have already explained why: he is an intelligent person, if he had been responsible, he would have prepared his answers beforehand instead of allowing himself to become frightened into stammering like a fool."

"And so?"

"If the hypotheses that we have considered are indeed correct, the number of suspects shrinks to three: the first, the musician, Smeaton: but how could he have managed it, against a man twice his size? Here too we would need to discover the means."

Philip listened to her in silence.

"The second, George Boleyn: but what link could there have been between the two? The one a gentleman, the other, that poor creature Crooks. Besides, Boleyn would have used poison, or a dagger. Or better still, would have hired an assassin, who would have struck from behind. As far as we can see, if indeed there is a motive – to save the Queen from blackmail – there is no opportunity, and if there is opportunity, there is no means."

Lady Constance looked at Philip. "And finally there remains Lady Alice. It is her being a suspect that torments you?"

As she spoke, her heart broke at the desperate expression which spread across the young man's face.

"If you only knew."

London, Palace of Whitehall
8 May 1536

At Whitehall, that evening, Sir Robert and his people gathered in their elegant white-walled, oak-beamed rooms.

Philip was the last to arrive: there were dark circles around his eyes, his shirt was rumpled and his hair untidy. "Lady Constance will have told you," he began. "We know that you wish to marry her," interrupted Sir Robert abruptly.

"But how can you think of spending your life with a woman whom you suspect of murder? Of sleeping in the same bed, of having children with? And when was it that you first had doubts about her? And why did you not speak to me about it?"

In replying Philip sounded as tired as he looked. "As I fell more and more in love, she every day seemed to push me away. 'I don't deserve you' she kept on saying. 'If only you knew.' Knew what, I wondered. I thought that she might have had a relationship before meeting me, which I could have accepted. But she did not want to say any more. I felt that she was carrying a secret burden; there was some kind of sadness within her. Dignified, fragile, she was struggling alone against something of which I could make no sense. I spoke of this to Lady Constance, I began to have doubts. All of which is… horrible."

It was distressing to see Philip cry, his face buried in his hands, his body collapsed on the bench like a set of discarded clothes. The others exchanged stricken glances; Margery approached him and stroked his head: if her only son had lived, he would have been Philip's age.

"Poor lad," said Sir Robert at length. "How upsetting for you. Nevertheless, I must tell you that in the last few days I have been making further enquiries and have realized several things. For instance, that Lady Alice is at least two spans taller than the victim, meaning that she could have struck Crooks on his head from above. That, while apparently fragile, she has the strong hands of someone who has ridden a lot and has hunted with bow and arrow, which would have rendered capable of wielding the candlestick. And if that pig Crooks had been threatening her, we would have the motive too."

"The means and the motive. But the opportunity?" demanded Philip.

"On the night of the treasure hunt, Crooks left the Queen's room before the others, knowing that Lady Alice would be going to that bedroom to fetch a candle. He followed her, perhaps surprised her. She grabbed the candlestick and defended herself, and in this case her self-defence would be legitimate and a good lawyer could save her from the gallows."

"And so?"

We shall do all we can for her, we will pay for the best defence counsel: but in order to proceed, we need to know the truth."

The windows were open to the scents of a summer evening, and at intervals could be heard the cries of seagulls wheeling over the river.

"Tomorrow," concluded Sir Robert, "we must clarify Barefoot's position, then we must call her again."

There was nothing further to say, and they separated in silence.

For the king's pharmacy

London, Palace of Whitehall
9 May 1536

Simon Barefoot did not appear before Sir Robert and his assistants until late in the morning: a long search throughout the palace by Sir Nicholas' guards had eventually flushed him out in the cellars, where he was found squatting on top of a large grain barrel, his bony arms wrapped around his knees.

"Master Barefoot, what a pleasure to see you again. And how do your studies on herbs and poisons progress?" Sir Robert asked pointedly.

The man did not reply, but stayed with his head down, his cassock rumpled, his eyes red as if painful in the light, his hair dishevelled.

Sir Robert continued: "We have learnt that you contrived to enter the room where the murder was committed. Would you mind explaining how you managed that?

"There is a door in the kitchen, which opens into a corridor leading to the bedroom. That's how I got in."

"We know that. Were you searching for something?"

The man was embarrassed. "William had entrusted me…"

"William Crooks?"

"Yes, he had written a letter, and I went to look for it."

"Why?

"It might have been compromising. William was my friend and I wanted to protect his reputation."

"Isn't it rather the case that you both used that route in order to spy on Lady Alice and her companion? And then you became jealous of Crooks, followed him along the passage, attacked him from behind and killed him?"

The man seemed unsettled, and kept twisting the hem of his cassock. He was sweating, his eyes rolling all around, he started crying. "Sir," he addressed himself to Sir Robert. "William and I grew up together in a small village. We were both poor, the children of servants. Then his mother was taken on at court as a washer-woman, and he managed to enter the King's service; as soon as he could, he had me join him. 'Simon' he said, 'can you prepare medicines for the royal pharmacy?' I had a basic knowledge of medicinal herbs, nothing more, but I said that I could: it meant having warm clothes and enough food to eat. So it was that the King's doctor took me as his assistant. I owed everything to William."

The man seemed sincere, and touching in his unexpected expression of loyalty.

Sir Robert continued: "It is rumoured that Crooks was blackmailing the Queen. The letter that you were looking for, what do you know about it?"

"Even if that were true, do you think that I would talk about it? You will learn nothing from me. I have never betrayed a friend. Let Will rest in peace."

Sir Nicholas got up, came round to the other side of the table and stood in front of Barefoot: an imposing figure in comparison with the little man. "Perhaps a spell in the Tower dungeons…"

Barefoot went very pale.

Sir Nicholas continued: The law prescribes: '*Peine forte et dure*'. Do you know what that means? 'Severe, painful torture.' When an accused man refuses to talk, they undress him, chain him stretched out on the floor, place sharp stones under his back and an axle across his chest, on top of which day by day are placed heavier and heavier stones. No food or water until he declares himself either innocent or guilty. And if he refuses to speak, he will die from suffocation or from his bones splintering inside him."

Barefoot knew about that torture. He hesitated. "William had learned something about the Queen," he stammered, "and he was blackmailing her. But he has paid for it, terribly, dying the way he did. I know nothing more than this, I swear it, I don't know anything else."

Sir Robert was persuaded that the man had told the truth and sent him away. But the complacent expression faded from his face when Lady Constance declared dryly: "He was lying. Did you notice how his body relaxed when you told him that he could go? He was sure that he had deceived you, he pretended to be beaten, but his eyes were bright, confident he had tricked you."

"His confidence will not last long," said Sir Robert. He gestured to Sir Nicholas, who went out into the corridor and grabbed Barefoot by the arm. "Come back in, we have some more questions to put to you."

Where was the letter hidden?

London, Palace of Whitehall
9 May 1536

Barefoot sat down again in front of Sir Robert. "I don't understand," he complained. Sir Robert banged his fist down on the table. "On the contrary, you understand very well. It is about that the paper that you stole from the room of Lady Alice."
"Sir Robert, I..."
Sir Nicholas came up beside him and began to squeeze his neck in a grip like iron. Barefoot struggled to free himself. "What do you want? I have told you that I was only trying to defend a friend's good name."
"Where was the letter hidden?"
He hesitated. Another tight squeeze around the neck: "In a panel behind the bed," he croaked, a white froth at the side of his mouth.
"Give it to me."
Against his will the man drew from his cassock a crumpled sheet, faded yellow, which he perhaps kept with him for future use. Sir Nicholas passed it to Sir Robert, who read it aloud: "George, this is the end. It's a tragedy for us. The son who might have saved

us…" He spread the sheet on the table, tried to smooth it out with his fingers. "This is the Queen's writing, that is certain. Desperate words. I can't make out the next part, there are some marks. There is a note at the bottom. It is written in another hand: crude handwriting, very uneven."

He adjusted his glasses and went on: 'This is why, my lady, you had better say nothing and pay me.'

He paused. "There's no doubt: this last sentence has been written by Crooks, they are his words."

He cleared his throat: "Simon Barefoot: it is clear that in one of your night-time visits to the ladies' room you lost this sheet, and one of them found and hid it. But the question is: how did you come to have it?"

"I'll never betray a friend," was the reply. He could not be made to say any more, Sir Robert had to let him leave. "Go on then, but if I were you, I should not expect to sleep soundly tonight."

When Barefoot had left, Margery commented: "Not to be trusted, people like that don't change."

"Well said," commented Lady Constance. She approached her husband: "How did you know that the paper was hidden in that room?"

"Instinct, my dear." Under no circumstances would he have admitted that he had just made a wild guess. But the thought of Barefoot worried him: what was he plotting under the cover of all his lies?

"They'll all be executed."

London, Palace of Whitehall
12 May 1536

While the tragedy of Anne Boleyn and her supposed lovers was running its course, life at the royal palace of Whitehall seemed halted, as in a painting. Visits by ambassadors had become rare, no more state banquets, parties and dances, few appearances by the sovereign, and all a mad spiral of speculation:

"The news today is that Norris, Weston, Brereton and Smeaton have been tried."

"Where?"

"In Westminster Hall."

"And found guilty, even if they have denied it."

"Apart from the musician, he confessed – but under torture."

"They'll all be executed."

"Norris, Weston and Brereton on the block; Smeaton isn't high-born, he'll face a traitor's death. Hanged, taken down from the gallows while still alive, his entrails burnt before his eyes, and the body eventually quartered."

"Because we are good Christians, in other countries they stuff the guts down their throats."

On the morning of the twelfth of May, accompanied by Mistress Holland, Lady Alice once more sat in front of Sir Robert. "Where is Philip?" she whispered in Bessie's ear.

"At the same table as Sir Robert, and Sir Nicholas is seated with them."

"Who else is in the room?"

"Lady Constance and her governess. I hope that they let me stay too."

"Philip, how does he look?"

"Unsettled."

"Sad?"

"Yes."

Lady Alice was wearing a pale green dress, with a rather high neckline, and no headdress on her fine silky hair, which hung loosely down her back, as befitted an unmarried woman. She adjusted the folds of her gown and clasped her hands together, as if in prayer. She looked younger than her years, and calm, unlike Sir Robert, who appeared anxious, and Sir Nicholas, who was sullen, Lady Constance and Margery, both downcast, and Philip, desolate.

There was a heavy silence, but someone had to speak. It was Sir Robert who began: "Lady Alice, this is Robert Kytchyn speaking to you, you know my voice. Here in London, at the moment, distressing events are taking place, yet it is my duty to try and shed some light on the matter of the late William Crooks. Could you please tell us something about him?"

There was no immediate response, several moments passed. Finally: "He had made me proposals. But I found them quite unacceptable. Not so much because of our difference in wealth and rank: in my situation the protection of a gentleman would have been welcome, even if he had been of modest background and means. But he was not a gentleman. I knew it instinctively: some things one knows by intuition even when not seen. The voice, the tone, the emphasis given to certain words. At once I felt sickened."

She paused, then repeated: "He was not a gentleman, Bessie confirmed that for me. Then he began writing to me, the letters that you have seen. I felt that he was spying on me, and when I was alone – I know my way around the Queen's rooms, I can't always be calling on Bessie – he used to follow me, press me against the wall, cover my mouth with his stinking hand and whisper obscene things to me: 'You would enjoy yourself in bed with me' was the cleanest. But he was close to the Queen, what could I do? Some time before that, one evening, I had had to struggle to free myself from him. I managed to escape, and when I arrived in the Queen's rooms, in tears, my dress torn, she put her arms around me: 'Alice, my dear child, what has happened to you? Who did this to you?' I told her. Then she murmured: 'I no longer have any power over him.' "

"I have nothing more to say…"

London, Palace of Whitehall
12 May 1536

No-one spoke, and in the quiet of the room could be heard the cries of the boatmen and the lapping of the water against the wharves.

"What happened next?" asked Sir Robert.

Lady Alice lowered her head. "I have nothing more to say."

Sir Robert remained silent, perhaps in the hope that she would feel compelled to speak again. But in the end he had to proceed:

"So it is I that shall tell you, even though it pains me to have to do so."

And he remembered how his wife had glanced sharply at him after the first questioning of the young woman, when he and Sir Nicholas had excluded her from the list of suspects. 'How could a girl, blind, delicate…' he had said that day.

Sir Robert repeated: "I shall tell you. It was the twenty-third of April, the day after the court had moved to Hampton Court because several cases of sweating sickness had been confirmed in London. The

Queen organized an entertainment for a few members of her close circle, there was treasure hunt too. Crooks knew that you were to fetch a candle. He waited for you in the corridor, came up to you and pushed you into a room: by chance it was yours. What happened next is for you to tell us."

Lady Alice raised her hands to her face. "I have nothing more to say."

"Then you grabbed a candlestick and brought it down on his head, from the front and from above, several times, at random. You are tall, young, strong in the arms. You bolted the door in order to delay discovery. You were familiar with the disposition of the furniture in the room and knew that there was a lawn underneath the window: with the help of a stool you climbed over the window sill and jumped down. But a purple thread got caught on the plaster inside the window."

Sir Robert stood up, took the thread out of his purse, placing it briefly between her fingers. Without removing his eyes from her, he continued: "You have a tunic of this colour, and the thread matches the material. That night it had been raining and the grass was wet. You crossed the lower courtyard and re-entered the Queen's rooms. Without the candle: you didn't have it, because it had rolled under one of the chests, where we found it."

He retrieved the thread from the young woman's hands. "Thank you. You were the last to return. I have made careful enquiries: you were out of breath,

Mistress Holland told me, you asked her if you were presentable. 'Your shoes are soaking,' she replied. You told her that you had come in from the courtyard. It was evening, in the torchlight she did not notice the bloodstains that were probably on your dress, and you gave it to the washerwoman the next day: it was soiled with wine and food, you said."

Lady Alice shook her head again, slowly. Philip rose, ashen and hollow-eyed. He kneeled down in front of her, breathing in the scent of lavender on her clothes. "Alice, my love," he murmured. "I beg you, say something."

She bent down towards him, and whispered in his ear: "Would you still love me if I confessed to being a killer?" She raised his face between her hands, and kissed him on the lips: a gentle kiss, but given as a sign of farewell.

'Peine forte et dure'

London, Palace of Whitehall
12 May 1536

Sir Robert's study at Whitehall was not large, but it was comfortable: a bookcase against the wall, a table with papers beneath the window, and stools with coloured cushions.

"So you are convinced that Lady Alice is guilty?" Lady Constance asked her husband when they were alone. While he was leafing through some papers, she seated herself on a bench beside the large stone fireplace.

"She is honest, she doesn't want to lie, and so she defends herself by saying nothing: but the evidence that we have and her silence speak in her place."

"And if she were to confess?"

"A good defence and a substantial sum of money paid into the Privy Purse would save her: but could Philip still love her? To what blackmail might she be exposed in the future? And there is something else: the Common Law provides that if she remains silent to the end, without having been found guilty, her goods will not be confiscated, and she can pass them on to whomever she wishes, perhaps even to Philip, whom she loves. She is an intelligent young woman and her blindness may give her strength greater than ours."

"In keeping quiet she is choosing death. It is as if she wanted to settle a debt, make amends at any cost."

"And leave to others the painful business of a decision."

A sparrow was perched on the window-ledge: he seemed to be watching them; it pecked at some grains, bobbed its head, then flew away.

Lady Constance went on: "Robert, what will happen now?"

"Juries are in a hurry these days. It will be *peine forte et dure* if she refuses to plead innocent or guilty."

"Might it not be claimed that she acted in a moment of madness?"

"She would be shut up at the Royal Bethlehem, at Bishopgate, the hospital for the insane. Do you know it? The people call it 'Bedlam', and it is real pandemonium inside. They chain up the inmates, beat them, give them rotten food to eat and make money by exhibiting them to the curious who come visiting."

"The alternative?"

"The prison at Newgate. Amongst women who have poisoned their husbands, drowned their own new-born, and drunkards, prostitutes, thieves. From that hell-hole there emerge only the dead or those taken on the cart to the gallows at Tyburn. Prisoners are not given food; they have to pay to have it. To talk with anyone inside you have to bribe the gaolers – a pack of rogues who trade on the misery of others: it's a penny merely to speak to a prisoner through the spy-hole."

"And so, what are you going to do?"

Sir Robert rested his elbows on the table, held his head between his hands, and closed his eyes. He seemed to have aged in the space of a few days.

"These are terrible times. The Queen shut up in the Tower, the accusations against her slanderous, her gentlemen condemned to death. What am I going to do? I shall continue with the investigation for as long as it seems worthwhile. Then I shall do my duty."

"Your duty? You mean to hand her over to the executioner? Send an innocent to the scaffold, if what you have supposed – it is just a matter of supposition, don't forget, without any proof – is untrue?"

"Without any proof?"

London, Palace of Whitehall
12 May 1536

"Without any proof?" Sir Robert retorted. "Do you know what made me sure that it was her? Crooks' skull and face had been smashed in, as if blindly. Whoever had seen bits of brain coming out of the poor man's head after the first blow would have realized that he was finished. But she did not see that, would not know whether it had hit the mark, whether or not it had been mortal. For that reason, with him still staggering around on his feet, she kept on striking at him: blindly, literally so in her case."

Lady Constance insisted: "Robert, the law states that guilt must be demonstrated beyond all reasonable doubt."

"It also states that someone found guilty must receive just punishment." He added: "I would have liked to save her and Philip from all that. I would have liked to spare those two young people that suffering. But it can't be helped; it can never be avoided by anyone."

"Can't it? I thought I knew you, Robert, I have loved you all these years. Why have you become so cynical, so stubborn? You disappoint me."

He looked at her disconsolately. He had agreed to undertake the enquiry on Nicholas' insistence, and in order not to spoil his reputation with the king. But also out of ambition, it was true. And now Norfolk's insistence that the investigation be brought to a speedy conclusion. But if Lady Alice was guilty, then it was his duty... 'Is there no saint in heaven to shield the young from life's iniquities?' he wondered. 'And if heaven has not moved a finger to help her, what can I be expected to do?'

Between them a moment of silence descended. Then the woman went to sit beside her husband, hugged him closely to her, he felt the tenderness, smelt the freshness of her cheeks and the scent of rose-water. "Robert, we have shared so much. Do you remember the happiness when our son was born? And the despair when we lost him? I hid my pain, you suffered in silence. But there are some sorrows that last for ever... Dear, even if Alice did kill, we know that it was not her fault. Why condemn her to death?"

"I don't..." Sir Robert began.

"Have you not thought of what might happen with time? I have. I was happy when those two fell in love. They would be close to us: their children, with celebrations at Christmas, birthdays, games, their little voices – all that would brighten our years to come..."

Somebody knocked. It was Sir Nicholas – he was wearing a breastplate and helmet. He remained on the doorstep: "Norfolk sent for me. He maintains that, in any case, Bessie Holland is not guilty, and that he will answer for her. So, if his lover is innocent, so is Lady Rochford, who was with her. Lady Lee is out of it, he says: as a friend of the Queen, why should she have removed the Queen's right-hand man?"

"Nicholas…"

"Let me finish. The other suspects are in the Tower, charged with much more serious offences. He is convinced, though, that there is sufficient evidence against Lady Alice, and that since his word is law, he has commanded that the case be closed and that I have her arrested."

Sir Robert approached him and placed a hand on his arm. "Nicholas…"

"I am sorry, Robert, but I must follow orders. This evening I shall be able to tell you more."

He left, his expression impassive: but why did he not come to the appointment that evening?

"She's called Nan Chetwood."

London, Palace of Whitehall
13 May 1536

As she had done since Constance was a baby, on the morning of the thirteenth of May, Margery prepared her bath: a tub, made of chestnut wood and quilted around the edges, was placed at the foot of the bed; jugs of boiling water were brought in, which she emptied into the tub, being careful not to wet the oak floorboards strewn with fragrant herbs; rolling up her sleeve, she tested the water with her elbow, poured in a little rosemary oil, and finally helped her mistress get into the bath.

But Margery was upset, and since Lady Constance seemed not to notice, she began to grumble more audibly. Finally she blurted out:

"Do you believe in death warnings?"

Constance looked at her. "What do you mean, Maggie?"

"They say that three knocks at the door are the sign of a coming death. Well, last night I heard three knocks at a door."

"It will have been the wind."

"There wasn't any wind."

"You must have dreamed it."

"I don't dream. I told the tallow-chandler's wife about it – we have become quite friendly – and she spoke of an old woman that she knows who has visions and foresees things. She helps women in labour, casts spells, reads the future. She lives in an alleyway near the quay. She's called Nan Chetwood."

"Superstition."

"I want to go there. It's next to the White Swan Inn, in Southwark."

"In Southwark? Among all the smugglers and prostitutes? Don't ask me to go with you and, make no mistake, you can't go there alone."

"If you don't want to come with me, I shall ask Philip."

So the following morning Margery and the young Philip left the Palace of Whitehall and proceeded cautiously towards Southwark, losing themselves several times in the alleyways and foul streets of the town. Every so often they saw pass a litter with a well-to-do lady inside, holding a bunch of sweet-smelling flowers to her nose. More than once Margery turned round with the feeling that they were being followed. The two of them passed by workshops belonging to goldsmiths, armourers, potters, lute-makers, apothecaries, saddlers and harness-makers, and finally arrived at London Bridge, full of shops, carts and townsfolk. Having crossed through the gardens of the priory of St Mary Overy, they made their way down the filthy riverside lanes – bustling with activity yet stinking of beer, horse-droppings, kitchen waste and lined with crumbling houses. Outside one of these a pair of kites fought over scraps with some little pigs, rose-pink under the crust of dirt which covered their bodies.

Death by water

London, Southwark
13 May 1536

Philip asked a passer-by how to reach the tavern that they were seeking. Then, curious, he asked what the circular building was upstream from London Bridge.

"I can see that you are from other parts," replied the man. "There every Sunday we have bear-baiting. It's always full of people; it costs a penny to stand and watch, and double under cover, in the gallery."

"What happens in these fights"

"There's a stake in the middle of the arena, there they tie the bear: but with a short rope so that he can't move very much. Then they let the dogs into the arena, English mastiffs for the most part, they circle the bear, and if they are trained for it, as not all are, they'll attack together. If the bear catches one of them with his claws, that's it, and the others back off; but if they can get in behind before he strikes, then it's usually over quickly. His teeth are filed down, of course, which makes it more even."

"Poor creature. It's only in this city that you see such barbarity!" grumbled Margery, as she and Philip set off in the direction that the man had indicated.

They arrived at a dilapidated door, painted blue, next to a crumbling building, the front of which was covered in ivy and from which hung a sign, rocking gently in the wind, showing a white swan on a green background. They knocked. The door was opened by a weary-looking girl with a faint scar on her one cheek: obviously the P of prostitute with which she had been branded when plying her trade in the city streets. In the room behind, a man, perhaps a merchant, held a young woman on his knees, and another two were standing close by, they were laughing and drinking beer.

When they asked for Nan Chetwood, the seer, the girl took them up a narrow spiral staircase and along an unlit corridor. Even the room that they were invited to enter was dark. Alongside one wall was a straw mattress, in a corner stood a copper brazier, no longer alight, and a single candle burned on the table; seated on a stool was an old woman with tangled grey hair and wrinkled arms. Her teeth were broken, but her eyes were alert, and Philip had the feeling that she could read his thoughts.

Margery began to speak: "We are here to…"

"I know why you are here. You are afraid and want to know more. You are despondent and want to know what will happen. But it's dangerous to look into the future."

She made them sit down on a bench in front of her. "Both of you, give me your hands," she demanded. She took them between her own, rested them on her knees and closed her eyes. Her nostrils dilated, as if she were smelling the air: "You are not his mother, but you are fond of him." She took hold of Philip's hands. "And you, boy, are suffering on account of someone who is precious to you."

'Is that all?' thought Philip. 'It's obvious that Margery is a maternal sort, but that we don't look alike, and it is not uncommon for someone of my age to be in love.'

As if she had heard him thinking aloud, the woman let go Margery's rough hand but kept hold of Philip's. Frowning, she remained motionless, eyes closed, breathing heavily as if asleep. "These are dark days," she muttered at last. "I see innocents on a scaffold, and blood, much blood. I see a sword coming down, a crown rolling into the straw. Tears and death. I see a death by water. A lonely death by water."

She shook herself as if waking from sleep. She did not want money. "Go away!" she said brusquely.

The two gave a coin to the girl and went out into the street, blinded by the bright morning light.

"Accusations against you, anonymous."

London, Palace of Whitehall
14 May 1536

"Lady Alice is being held in the prison at Newgate," said Sir Nicholas on entering Sir Robert's study. He threw some papers down on the table: "And my men brought me these this morning, they were collected from various taverns. Accusations against you, anonymous, gross lies, but they will do you harm."

Lady Constance picked up one of the sheets. "Here they write that you let a woman die, that you refused to treat her."

Sir Robert appeared grieved. He murmured: "It is an old story. The woman was dying of puerperal fever, nothing could be done. I told the husband to let her close her eyes in peace and to give his attention to the baby instead, who could survive. But this memory torments me, together with the thought that I might have been able to save her."

"You have never talked to me about it, Robert. Why not?"

"I was ashamed, it was a mark against me. I have asked God's pardon for it many times. I ask your pardon too."

"But who could know of this matter?" murmured Sir Nicholas. "That cursed Barefoot? So was he preparing blackmail? And then, look at these sheets: badly made by fourth-rate workers, on poor-quality paper and with ink that smudges. A cheap effort."

Lady Constance stood up. "Let us go into the garden," she suggested. "We can talk there without anyone being able to overhear."

The gardens of the royal residence of Whitehall had been appropriated by Chancellor Thomas Cromwell from the parish of St Margaret's and Westminster Abbey. They Laid out in terraces sloping down towards the river, they had fountains, fruit trees, a maze and, at the centre, on the ground, a large metal sundial, painted in different colours, showing the months and the phases of the moon.

The three sat down on a stone bench in the shade of an oak tree.

"Norfolk's orders were that I should escort Lady Alice to Newgate Prison," said Sir Nicholas, "and I had to obey. Bessie did nothing but keep hugging her and protesting about the injustice of the matter. She was furiously sewing coins into Lady Alice's gown: she does not realize that they will search her and remove anything of value, from her shoes to the rings on her fingers."

148

Lady Constance listened in dismay; Sir Robert twisted his hands together.

"To give her at least a night's respite, I have not yet issued the order for *peine forte et dure*. But I shall have to in a few days."

"Norfolk mustn't know."

London, Palace of Whitehall
14 May, 1536

At that moment they saw Margery and Philip approaching. She was leaning on his arm and speaking to him in an undertone. 'She is giving him a lecture' all three of them thought. She had a kind heart, but this often meant her inflicting on him numerous pieces of advice.

Without taking any notice of the men, Margery sank down on the bench next to Lady Constance and recounted in a single breath her visit to Southwark. And concluded: "Tears, blood, and a death by water, the woman said."

Sir Nicholas voiced his thoughts. "Anne Boleyn is to be tried. She'll certainly be found guilty, with all the dirty lies that they have concocted about her. A lot of blood will run, and innocents go to the gallows."

"The Queen, her gentlemen, even her brother. Norfolk will strive to save his own neck when the jury condemns his niece, but he too is bound to fall into disgrace, along with the Howards and the Boleyns," added Sir Robert.

"But why 'death by water'? Lady Constance asked her.

"At the time the woman probably had in mind Anne Boleyn, her boat-trip from Greenwich to the Tower. At high tide, there are dangerous whirlpools on the river, and it was night-time when she was taken to the fortress. But," he looked at Philip, "now we must do what we can for Lady Alice."

"Has she admitted anything?" asked Philip.

"No, but Newgate Prison is among the most brutal in the kingdom."

"And she is so delicate," said Philip.

All five of them were heavy-hearted, and Philip looked in turn at Sir Robert and Sir Nicholas, as if imploring help. Sir Robert was the first to speak: "My commission is still in force, Nicholas?"

"It has never been revoked. If it should be so in the future, I shall ensure that the letter to you on this matter goes astray. Without betraying myself, you understand. Now I bid you farewell, I must leave," and he went off in a hurry, as if aware of something that he chose not to mention.

Sir Robert collected his thoughts, then chose his words carefully: "I have some acquaintance with the London courts. Having been entrusted with the investigation by the King, I could take advantage of my position to visit the prison."

"Oh yes, Robert," Lady Constance whispered to him.

"To visit Lady Alice, bring her some comfort, seek to persuade her to say something in her own defence. That is what matters. Because if she does not declare herself either guilty or not guilty, the court will not even allow me to procure her a lawyer."

"Can I come with you?" begged Philip.

Sir Robert shook his head. "If they allow someone to go there with me, it will have to be a woman."

"Not Mistress Holland," said Lady Constance. "Beware: I think it is important that Norfolk knows nothing of our plans."

"So Margery will come." 'Norfolk mustn't know' thought Sir Robert. But he already knew a lot of things: the alibis of the suspects, the circumstantial details still to check, but above all the evidence regarding Lady Alice's guilt. Naturally he wanted to be kept informed, but who could have passed on these details? He tried to work out how much Bessie Holland might know, or indeed Sir Nicholas, always present at the meetings, with his usual impassive attitude. A suspicion began to grow in his mind, an inkling, a hint: that his friend was in some way personally involved in this story.

"The verdict had already been decided..."

Tower of London
15 May 1536

It was several days since Anne Boleyn's court had been dismantled, ladies in waiting, valets, servants taken away, a clear sign that her fate had already been decided. In the manor house at Chelsea, alongside the river, the King had installed the lady who would become his next wife, Jane Seymour. It was there that the royal barge headed every afternoon.

On 15 May Anne Boleyn was due to appear at the court set up in the Great Hall in the Tower, to be tried. After her it would be the turn of her brother George. More than two thousand people were present at the trial, and among them Lady Constance, Margery and Philip, who had come to London for a quite different purpose and now found themselves witnessing one of the darkest episodes in the history of the kingdom.

"It seems that among the Queen's papers they found a letter from a man in her circle, very compromising," said the plump wife of a merchant seated next to Lady Constance.

"From that William Crooks who was killed?" asked the latter casually. "And do they know what was written in it?"

"They say it related to the secret between her and her brother, about that child of theirs which was still-born."

Another woman interrupted: "That tale of incest. So it's true that the man was blackmailing her?"

"Not just for that. There are those who say that she did betray the King, that she hid her lovers in the large chests in her rooms and that they would spring out at night when the ladies and servants had left," the merchant's wife replied. "Last summer the Queen had announced that she was pregnant again. However, everyone saw that she remained slim and did not enlarge her clothes at all."

"And then?"

The woman continued, her eyes shining as she spoke, whilst others around her pricked up their ears. "The story goes that one evening the King had suddenly decided to go to his wife's rooms. He was in the hallway outside when he heard some frantic music. He threw open the door and found Anne dancing like someone possessed, pirouetting and jumping with her admirers. So the pregnancy was all a farce!

She paused for breath, then continued: "They say that the sovereign seized her by the arm and threw her to the ground. As her wrist was grabbed the sleeve went up, revealing a huge, hairy mole, the sign of a witch. So he…"

The woman halted: without a herald to announce her, Anne Boleyn, appeared in the hall, accompanied by the Governor of the Tower, Sir William Kingston.

On entering the Queen looked around. She had her hair gathered up in a headdress, in the French fashion with velvet and pearls, and was wearing a green velvet dress embroidered in gold. For a moment to Lady Constance it seemed to recall the banquet that had been held there to celebrate her coronation. It had been only three years before: now a jury of twenty-six peers called to try her were seated at a table, and none of these had stood up when she entered.

She paused, and looked each one of these in the face. She knew them all: Charles Brandon, the Duke of Suffolk, husband of the King's sister, who hated her. The Marquis of Exeter, and his cousin, Lord Montague, supporters of Queen Catherine; Lord Morley, another of Catherine's partisans; Henry Percy, to whom she had been betrothed prior to King Henry's abrupt invasion of her life. And then Worcester, Rutland, Sussex; and Dacre, the traitor, and Cobham, the guardian of the King's illegitimate son. All friends of the sovereign, and indebted to him in one way or another. And he, screened by a curtain, like a scorpion ready to inject its poison, watched and listened to all the proceedings.

"It is a grievous day indeed when the jurors of an English court do not rise to their feet at the entrance of their queen," said Anne Boleyn. Her manner was dignified, her voice sad.

One after the other the jurors stood up, including her uncle, the Duke of Norfolk, who presided over the jury. Foreign ambassadors and the dignitaries of the City, who were on the right of the jury, also stood up, as did ladies, merchants and the people of London, both men and above all women, who were facing them. At the end of the hall, in chains, were her purported lovers.

'What will those poor souls be thinking?' an unhappy Lady Constance wondered. 'And she, the Queen – those eyes of hers which once shone with pride now betray fear. And how anxious she must feel at the thought of the little Elizabeth.'

There was silence; the courtroom held its breath as Norfolk read the indictment.

"Lady Anne, whilst you were Queen of England you nursed malice against your most excellent husband and damaged his welfare. Led astray by demonic promptings and influenced by your own fleshly desires, you craved that numerous of the King's servants become your lovers. You seduced them with obscene talk and kisses and gifts, and with other unmentionable encouragements.

To be precise:

on the sixth of October 1533 and in the following days, in the Palace of Westminster, you seduced the Gentleman of the King's Bedchamber Henry Norris, with whom you had carnal relations;

156

on the twenty-seventh and twenty-eighth of November of the same year at Hampton Court you lay with William Brereton;

on the nineteenth of May, 1534, with Mark Smeaton;

on the twentieth of May and the twentieth of June of the same year with Francis Weston.

You have mocked the sovereign, describing him as impotent; you have declared that if he were to die, you would marry one of your lovers; you have seduced your own brother, hoping to have a child by him; you poisoned the dowager Princess Catherine, and sought to poison her daughter, Princess Mary.

If you confess your crimes, you may beg the King's mercy."

During the reading many of those listening recognized that the accusations were implausible, the dates and places false: it was known, for instance, that on the days cited, the Queen had been elsewhere and in different company, on official engagements at which the jurors themselves had even been present.

"Guilty,"they all said, one after the other

Tower of London
15 May 1536

The Queen rose and looking beyond the jury, appealed to the people. "You see before you a woman," she said, "defenceless against hostile men and a sentence which has already been passed. I deny every accusation: and, I ask you to judge, how I could be an adulteress if only yesterday Archbishop Cranmer declared this marriage of mine null and void?"

She paused, and a murmur in her favour arose within the crowd.

"I protest my loyalty to the king," she continued, "and I declare that my only fault is to have sometimes let myself be fired by jealous rage. I have not been able to close my eyes and keep quiet. I will know how to die a good death, if this will smooth the King's path towards a new happiness."

Lady Constance whispered in Margery's ear: "She is saying nothing against the King because she is trying to protect the little Elizabeth."

"They all know that she is innocent. They can't condemn her," responded Margery, also speaking in a low voice.

"They'll manage it, you'll see," said Philip, and there was anger in his voice. He was thinking: 'The King wants her dead, and will get his way. Norfolk wants Alice condemned in order to distract people from the wrongdoings of the King, and he will succeed in getting that too."

With a rustle of clothes and a scraping of feet, the members of the jury stood up. "Guilty," they said, one after the other, all twenty-six of them. Norfolk wept as he read out the verdict that doomed his niece.

"Anne Boleyn: you have been found guilty of high treason, adultery and incest, for which the penalty is death. You will be beheaded or burnt at the stake within these precincts, on Tower Green, according to the King's pleasure."

At the side of the jury stood a guard with the executioner's axe, the blade turned to the wall. It was now turned towards her. Many of the public, overcome by distress, left the room: among these were Lady Constance, Margery and Philip. The Governor of the Tower led Anne Boleyn back to her icy rooms.

One of the ladies who were with her during this time recounted how the Queen had received a last visit from Princess Elizabeth – the child would be three years old in September.

"Mama, do you have a present for me?" the little girl had asked her. She had taken from her neck the pearl necklace with the gold pendant, the **B** of Boleyn, the only piece of jewellery that she had been allowed to keep, and had put it in the small hands. Then she had

embraced her, with the passion of someone who is
about to leave for ever.

Newgate Prison

London, Southwark
16 May 1536

While Lady Constance was attending the Queen's trial,
Sir Robert sought to obtain a pass for Newgate Prison,
anxiously aware that his warrant might soon run out,
now that the Boleyns had fallen into disgrace. Spurred
on by a sense of discomfort at his wife's words, he
spent the entire day between the Chancery and the
Courts: at each step everyone sent him somewhere
else, after making sure to be paid. Only on the
morning of the sixteenth was he finally able to set out
with Margery to the place where Lady Alice was
imprisoned.

With the unusually hot weather of late, the level of the
Thames had gone down, exposing rotting remains of
all kinds along the riverbanks. When they arrived in
the Shambles, the butchers' quarter, the stench of
meat exposed to the sun and the rivulets of noxious
fluids that ran long the centre of the street made
Margery declare more than once they would never be
able to reach their destination. Eventually, having

161

made their way through Newgate market and passed Greyfriars Church, they arrived in Newgate Street, directly opposite the large square towers of the prison.

Sir Robert pounded hard with the heavy iron knocker on the main gate. A spy-hole opened. "I have a commission from the Duke of Norfolk, for the prisoner Alice Winter. There's a relative with me who will pay for the visit."

The door opened wide to reveal the pock-marked face of a gaoler. "Alice Winter, eh? The one who acts the lady." Having pocketed the money, the man gestured to his assistant: "Take them to the pit."

The latter led them along a corridor flanked by several narrow cells. Here, on straw-covered floors, sprawled men and boys, their wrists chained to the walls. Large cockroaches and enormous rats scurried about the visitors' feet, which made a crunching sound as they walked over the lice-covered ground; they could hardly breathe because of the overwhelming smell of urine and excrement. With the moaning and cries and hurled insults, the rattling of chains and clanging of doors, the din was deafening.

They passed then through another courtyard and along a second corridor. Here the prisoners were women: seated on straw, dishevelled, dressed in rags but without chains, hands stretched out through the bars, begging for a little money 'for the love of God, to keep us from starving'. They gave them a few coins. The gaoler lit a torch and guided them down a spiral staircase, which led to a dungeon. He opened the barred door, ushered them in, remaining outside. "I'll wait on the stairs," he said. He locked the door and took away the key and the torch.

"So you are guilty?"

London, Southwark
16 May 1536

The 'pit' was a dark hole barely lit by the few glimmers of light that passed through a grill. As icy as the rest of the prison, the walls glistened with water, the filthy straw giving off a foul, intolerable odour, with insects everywhere on the ground and in the air.

Lady Alice was huddled up in a corner, barefoot, her arms around her knees. When she heard them enter, she raised her head: "Philip?" she murmured.

Guided by that faint voice, Margery groped her way forwards: "It's Sir Robert and I," she said. She sat down next to Alice and put her arms round her; Alice put her head on Margery's shoulder. She had dark shadows under her eyes and her delicate face was frightened and tired. "Oh, Margery," she sighed.

Margery put down the bag that she had brought with her and took out a cloth, on which she poured rose water, proceeding to clean Alice's face and hands and to comb her hair. They noticed that she was shivering: Sir Robert took off his cloak and put it around her shoulders; she pulled it close. "Thank you," she said, her eyes, expressionless, turned towards them.

So Margery pulled out a parcel of bread and meat, which she placed in the other's hands. "Come, eat," she ordered, and the girl obeyed – she was clearly hungry. Just as avidly she also drank some light beer from a flask that the woman passed to her.

They heard the door open. "Your time's over," said the gaoler. Sir Robert took him by the arm and went out into the corridor. "What's your name?" he asked.

"Thomas Scarcliff, sir."

"Are you the one in charge of this prisoner?" he asked. The man nodded. Sir Robert saw his empty eye socket, his ugly face, covered in warts: but he had to make a friend of him. He took from his belt a small money-bag and passed it to him. Scarcliff weighed it in his hand. He smiled, revealing a row of holes where his teeth had been. "At your service, sir. Take as much time as you want. I'll leave the torch with you."

"I shall be coming again in the next few days, together with some people from the court: she used to be a lady-in-waiting to the Queen. If an order to torture her should come, I would ask you to delay it as long as possible."

"You'll have to speak to the head gaoler about that. You'll need money."

"That won't be lacking," promised Sir Robert. "And there'll be more for you too."

Sir Robert came back in. Margery was holding Alice in her arms, rocking her like a child. Alice was smiling, her eyes closed. She seemed to him even more beautiful like that. He crouched down beside her. "Lady Alice, tell me something," he asked softly.

"What."

"I think you know that if you plead neither innocent nor guilty I won't even be able to provide you with legal counsel."

"I know."

"Then why do you create these problems for me? And for you it will be the stones, loaded onto you until your spine snaps or you suffocate. A slow death. So painful that you will beg to be hanged. Tell me: you're not shielding anyone, are you?"

"I have nothing more to say: I beg you, don't ask me anything further, don't torment me. And don't torment yourself. As far as I am concerned, to die will be to clear a debt."

"So you're guilty?"

"It's not matter of guilt. I've done nothing wrong."

Her voice was calm. She was silent. She passed her hands over her face. "What a lovely scent, Margery: I've always loved rose water."

She turned her face towards Sir Robert. "I beg you, tell me about the Queen."

"She's been tried."

"And...?"

"Condemned."

"They'll banish her from court?"

166

"She's been condemned to death. The King will decide, between the stake to punish her incest, and the block, as revenge for her betrayal."

"They will be killing an innocent. A woman who in her own way loved him. What disillusion." She clasped her hands together. "May Heaven have pity on her!"

She was silent again. Then: "As for me, I would only like to see Philip, for one last time."

They left the cell, saddened by her words. Sitting on the bottom step of the spiral staircase, the gaoler was counting his money.

"Do you plead guilty or not guilty?"

London, the High Court
17 May 1536

The London assizes and petty sessions were being held outside the city walls, near to Newgate. On the morning of the seventeenth of May the courtroom in which Lady Alice would appear was already crowded. The first to be tried would be those being prosecuted for minor offences, then those destined for the scaffold: murderers, child rapists, those who had stolen goods worth more than a shilling, highwaymen. And all brought in with them an odour of prison and of fear.

The judge, wrapped in his scarlet cape, had clear eyes, thin lips and great haste. He informed the jurors that they would remain locked in a room without food or drink until they reached unanimous verdicts: for which reason a young prostitute was swiftly condemned to a public whipping outside the vestry of Old St Paul's, whilst her protector was to have his ears cut off; a young boy, who gazed around confusedly, as if not sure why he was there, was to be branded on the base of his thumb with T for thief. So too a couple of cattle thieves were rapidly dispatched to the gallows at Tyburn, along with a highwayman: at Tyburn the gallows had been deliberately constructed by the City authorities so that money could be saved by hanging three offenders at a time.

Also condemned to die was a pirate – the English Channel was infested with them. The sentence would be carried out in the harbour at Wapping. There the gibbet, erected at the level of the low tide, would bring a slow death as the water gradually rose. After a few days the body would be removed, covered in pitch and exposed on one of the arches of London Bridge as a deterrent to others.

A woman who had slandered her husband was subjected to the 'scold's bridle', a small cage strapped over the head, the sharp blade of which fitted in her mouth, cutting her tongue every time that she tried to speak; a riotous drinker was condemned to wear a 'drunkard's coat', a barrel from which only the hands and feet emerged: he would be obliged to walk dressed in this way through the streets of his neighbourhood, while the inhabitants made fun of him.

As for the young pickpocket, the judge ordered: "Brand him immediately so we can be sure that the sentence is carried out and that no bribery is used to obtain a cooler iron." The room was suffused with the smell of burning flesh.

Lady Alice's moment arrived. She was wrapped in Sir Robert's cloak, and accompanied by the jailer, now respectful after being given money.

The judge raised his eyes from his papers and looked at the young woman, so out of place in such surroundings.

"Alice Winters of Broughton Astley," he said, "Maid of Honour to the Queen. You are accused of the murder of a certain William Crooks, a servant of the Court. Do you plead guilty or not guilty?"

"I do not wish to reply, sir," she said in a clear voice.

This declaration was surprising: all those who had been tried so far had sworn that they were innocent.

"And why not, if I may ask?"

She was silent for a moment, her hands clasped together, eyes lowered. "I am not afraid to die."

"Do not be foolish, madam. Why risk your life, if one word were enough to save it?"

"It is the old who struggle to survive. I have already had my life, my happiness. My young love."

'Words directed at me,' thought Philip, his heart burning. 'She knows that I am here. She is resigned to die; there is no more hope."

"Robert Kytchyn, a charlatan!"

London, Court of the King's Bench
17 May 1536

Sir Robert, seated next to him on the front row, and until that moment apparently unmoved, rose and approached the judge's bench. He showed him the paper attesting to his commission: "I am a doctor, the investigator charged by the Duke of Norfolk to lead the enquiry into the death of William Crooks, the Queen's personal assistant. I have the sovereign's confidence, as my lord the Duke will testify."

The judge examined the document. "Yes, I remember you, Sir Robert Kytchyn. You teach at Cambridge. I have read some of your treatises with interest."

"You are most kind. I have carried out an investigation at the Court of Whitehall, and I have serious doubts about the guilt of the accused, not least given the fact that she is blind, as you can see. I ask for time to undertake further enquiries, and that meanwhile the young lady be allowed to remain at liberty. I shall ensure that she is kept under surveillance."

The judge returned the paper: "An additional period of investigation: certainly, if you feel that it is necessary."

There arose a voice from among the people present in the courtroom. On his feet a little man with straight white hair was shaking his fist and shouting: "Charlatan! Yes, ladies and gentlemen, Sir Robert Kytchyn is a charlatan. He has no mandate and does not enjoy the king's confidence! His protector, Norfolk, no longer has any authority: he was taken to the Tower this very morning. He says that he is acting on behalf of the Queen, a whore condemned to the scaffold. Investigator, my hat! Shame on you for trying to deceive the court!"

The judge turned to Sir Robert. "How much of this is true?"

"Up to now no-one has annulled my commission. I am only trying to do my duty."

Looking in the other's eyes, the judge saw only an honest man, one racked by doubt.

"I understand you. And, believe me, I sympathize with you. However, as matters stand, I must postpone all decisions. Alice Winters will remain in Newgate, and must appear again in this court in two weeks' time. You have the permission of the court to continue with your enquiries." He added in an undertone: "Take as much advantage of the mandate as you can while it still holds good."

He turned to the little man, who was still standing, purple in the face. "You down there, what is your name?"

"Simon Barefoot, my lord." He looked around with an air of importance, flaunting himself in an elegant cloak. "I am the assistant to the court doctor."

"Indeed. Since you have disturbed the orderly procedure of this hearing, I rule that you be condemned to thirty days' hard labour, to take the particular form of cleaning the cells and latrines in the Tower dungeons on a daily basis. My decision is final," he concluded, and left the courtroom leaving Barefoot open-mouthed and aghast while the people behind him sniggered, and others applauded Sir Robert.

While Sir Robert and his company were leaving the court they heard the bell ring from St. Sepulchre's, the church attached to the High Court, as always happened when there was an execution. Later they ran into a large rabble which was making its way back from the scaffold on Tower Hill, having watched the beheading of four of Anne Boleyn's alleged lovers. The fifth, her brother, would have been dispatched within the precincts of the Tower, as befitted his rank. The crowd had broken up into small groups.

"They all declared that they were innocent," one of them commented.

"They climbed up on the platform, spoke a few words, then the show began," said another.

"Do you remember the time that the headsman didn't manage to finish the job and held out the axe and some money to anyone who would help him. That's what happened to William Norris: the axe chopped off his shoulder, then it got stuck in the wood and after several more blows, they had to end it with a knife."

"Blood spouting everywhere, and bits of bone."

"They gathered up the pieces and put them in a basket, cleaned down the block, and then on with the next one."

"Careful, I can see some of the king's men, we'd better be off."

A troop of soldiers galloped into the lane, splashing mud over bystanders, who had to press back against the house walls to avoid getting knocked down.

'If in doubt, say nothing.'

Streets of London
17 May 1536

It had been raining all night: the waters of the Thames were now running swiftly, a pleasant breeze arose from the river, people were coming and going about their business, groups of children were playing in the streets. During the journey to the palace at Whitehall Sir Robert and his company was each of them deep in their own thoughts.

'The commission has not been annulled, take advantage of that' the judge had said. But the question of how best to do so tormented Sir Robert. *'In dubiis abstine'*. If in doubt, do nothing, suspend judgement. In fact, what proof did he have? The woollen thread? The real murderer could have put it there himself. The sodden shoes? What wrong was there in her having crossed the courtyard rather than gone along the corridor that night? But why would she not speak? Perhaps she thought that someone dear to her was involved and wished to protect them. *'In dubiis pro reo'*. Sir Nicholas, his friend, had had no doubts. A mistake, yes, it had been a mistake to request his assistance in the investigation. He had not been there in court that morning. Why did he no longer show himself? Was he out of favour too? Or implicated in some way in the murder?

Walking beside the others, his hands thrust deep in the pockets of his tunic, Philip had a single thought: to see Alice, clasp her in his arms, save her. To try anything, however fanciful. Yes, escape from prison. Money was needed, a lot. Lady Constance: she would help. And Margery, of course. Dear old Margery, she would give up her savings without hesitation. He and Alice would flee. A quiet place, a village in the North. Make a new life, start again. The sheltered vales of Yorkshire? Too risky, anywhere in England they would be found. France was safer. Yes, France...
And he pictured to himself the golden fields full of sunflowers, and the broad skies, and the winds of Normandy.

Margery would have liked to go back to the gaol, quickly, immediately. To take Alice some food and clean underclothes. A bit of common sense, that's what was needed in this world. Eating and getting clean brings cheer. Poor Philip, he must be heartbroken. How fortunate that each should fall in love with the other at the same time – it rarely happens like that. But what a price to pay: yet, one pays for everything in this life. Alice had recognized the scent, rose-water, which she liked. Some nice rich meat broth, that would do her good. But what was the point if she was condemned to death?

Lady Constance's thoughts had turned to her husband. That morning, in court, he had run a great risk. Arrest even, for contempt of court. That Barefoot, she would have liked to strangle him with her own hands, squash him under her heel like a foul beetle, wipe him from the face of the earth. But no, the fault was all hers. It had been her, her prattling: children, the years to come. Stupid, stupid. Enough, she would not open her mouth again. At least, not regarding Alice. And while she was walking she felt she wanted to embrace him, to hold him close, her man.

An accidental death

London, Newgate
17 May 1536

On this occasion it was Sir Robert and Philip who took themselves to Newgate, with a sack of food, a gown and fresh linen which Margery had prepared. The gaoler turned the key in the lock, they went in the cell. "Alice," said Philip. She looked up at him, radiant, and stretched out her hands. He took her in his arms. But she drew back, suddenly aware of her unkempt appearance and her smell: but Philip held her fast, passed a hand through her hair and down her slender neck. "You are beautiful," he whispered. Philip held her in his arms, a moment dreamed of for days. He kissed her face gently; she let him do so, seriously, like a thoughtful child.

They sat down on the straw, she wanted news of Margery, Bessie, Lady Constance.
"And the Queen?" she asked finally.
"She's shut in the Tower. They say that she weeps when she thinks of the fate of the little Elizabeth. Otherwise, she's resigned."

"I was fond of her."

Now she rested her head against his shoulder.

"Alice, Sir Robert has explained to you. If you continue to keep silent, you too will be condemned to death. It's the law."

She raised her face towards his, grown thin and more mature in these few days. "Don't think that I am anxious to die."

"Well then, why?"

"Perhaps death is not the worst thing that can happen to me…"

She said this with a calm smile, though her words wounded Philip like a knife.

Sir Robert, who had prepared a series of questions to put to her – well rounded, logical, cogent – stood back, then nodded to the guard and went out with him into the corridor.

"I've got a daughter that age too," said the man.

"She is not my daughter; we didn't have any children. But the boy lives with us, I am his tutor."

"The girl, what's she done?"

"I wish I knew."

"There's a man's death in it, I've heard. But how is it possible with one so lovely, so young?"

Sir Robert thought a moment. "You said your name was Scarcliff, didn't you?"

"Thomas Scarcliff, sir."

"Well, Thomas, listen. If the boy should ask you…"

He hesitated.

"Ask me what, sir?"

179

"I don't know, anything: well, be assured that you would be well paid."

"Something   risky?"

"I've really no idea. I just mentioned it. But remember what I said."

Sir Robert came back in the cell. "Did you tell her?" he asked Philip in a low voice. The latter shook his head. "I promised her that I would return tomorrow."

"It's better that she has some idea."

"Time to get things ready."

"I don't wish to know about it, but whatever you are thinking of doing, do it quickly."

They re-entered Whitehall through the gardens, and Lady Constance came out to meet them.

"Barefoot is dead," she announced.

"What? It's not possible!" exclaimed Sir Robert. "When, how?"

"He hadn't been seen around for several days, they found him this morning in his laboratory. On the floor, all yellow, his mouth full of blood. There were deadly herbs and toadstools on the shelves, coloured liquids in glass vessels – he was engaged in some studies, they say, and it seems that he poisoned himself while carrying out one of his experiments."

"He might have been killed, perhaps by someone who wanted to prevent him saying something. We know that the dead don't speak."

Lady Constance took her husband's arm and the three of them made their way towards the palace. In a voice a little above a whisper: "Robert," she said, "I have been afraid for you. Jealousy made that man seek to do you harm, and that can't be ignored just because he's dead."

At this, to the amazement of the other two, Philip burst out: "Nor pardoned. Think how he behaved with the Queen. And of his wickedness and treachery towards you – you haven't forgotten the poisoned beer, have you?" And though usually moderate in his judgements, he added: "That man was a nobody, he was a fool when living, and it is only right that he died by his own hand, by accident."
"Amen," intoned Lady Constance.

"We would all be risking our necks."

London, Whitehall
17 May 1536

Daniel Lewis, the King's head cook had had some choice dishes prepared for lunch: soup made from onions soaked in almond milk, pork loin roasted in cumin and red wine, fish in a spicy sauce, a pudding of quince steeped in honey and nutmeg.

Sir Robert and his party dined in the great hall together with few courtiers, and made no reference to the events of the morning; later too, in their rooms, they maintained a heavy silence, pondering their various thoughts. Lady Constance and Margery settled to some darning at the window, Sir Robert sat at his table, striving to read some notes, and Philip was seated by the marble hearth, torturing himself over what to do.

"But there are a lot of people granted a royal pardon," Margery finally blurted out. "Why not her?"

Sir Robert rubbed his temples with his fingers: "Because she would have to plead guilty or not guilty, as the law demands. But she might be shielding someone, that's the problem.

He muttered: "Two weeks, more investigations: but where, how, who else can be questioned after having listened to everyone, and to the gossip and slanders, even that of the cooks and servants?"

Philip turned to him: "I have something to say." He hesitated. "Sir Robert, perhaps it is better that you don't hear."

"Talk away, I shan't listen." And he gave a sad smile.

"Given that she will not speak, because she is stubborn – she has driven me mad with her silences – the only way out is," here he lowered his voice, "that we help her escape from prison."

Lady Constance and Margery stared at him: the suggestion had something to commend it. Sir Robert, on the other hand, was alarmed: "We? Do you realize what you are saying?"

Quietly Lady Constance commented: "It is for that reason that I would ask you to stay out of it."

"We would all be risking our necks, do you understand?"

"Robert, don't worry. Wouldn't it be best, first of all, to go back and see that young lady? Talk to her, make her see sense. She might have reflected and…"

"So, she is to die."

London, Palace of Whitehall
17 May 1536

"Perhaps she has reflected. But don't you see?" lamented Sir Robert. "All of you have answers. All, except me. Everyone has peace of mind. Except me."

There was a rustling sound as, seated at his table, he smoothed out some papers with his fingers. Lady Constance went to sit at his side, putting an arm around his bent shoulders, aware of his distress. As often when she sought to comfort him, she spoke in a forthright fashion. "Now don't keep on complaining, my dear. You are not the only one suffering, don't forget that."

"The terrible thing is not knowing what actually happened. There is what is called justice. You must see that I, as the King's servant in this matter…"

"That's enough of your tormenting us. Stop complaining about your situation. And stop dressing in black: you look like a sexton. The time has come to do something."

"Do what? I don't want to know anything about it, and you three, all of you, pay heed to the risks that you are running."

He moved away from her, brusquely, and returned to looking at his papers. "Dressed like a sexton," he muttered.

With the shrewdness of the woman who has long been married, Lady Constance did not reply but went to sit next to Philip. "Philip, tell me your plans," she asked quietly.

"To flee to France. In England we shall always be in danger."

'Farewell to a future with them, to children's laughter in the house,' thought Lady Constance. She bit her lip, raised her head. "France would certainly be safer. You would have to secure passage on some ship," she said.

"Any ship, providing it left soon," said Philip.

Margery fetched a pair of scissors from the embroidery drawer, hurriedly unpicked the hem of her linen underskirt and withdrew some money. "Take this, to pay for the crossing. It is all I have."

Philip put his hand on hers and squeezed it, without saying anything.

Sir Robert lifted his eyes from the notes that he was feigning to read: "What would you pay the gaolers with?"

"With my money," replied Lady Constance. She explained to Philip: "Sir Robert left me in possession of my properties when we married, and I never travel without money."

185

She got up, approached the wall beside the fireplace and moved aside a brick, revealing a shallow recess, from which she took out a small casket: it contained coins and some jewellery.

Sir Robert came up to her, put his hand in and withdrew it full of silver coins, then let them drop back in, with a sharp jingle. "There won't be enough here."

The three others looked up at him. "No, there won't be enough. There's the gaoler, Scarcliff, the one with the warts. He's already had some money, but he'd want more. Then there's the captain of the guards, he would demand a great deal for not reporting it. You would have to pay in gold coin, and so that he didn't betray you, you would have to promise him the same sum again if everything went well."

Lady Constance looked him in the eyes. "So, she is to die," she murmured.

He looked at himself in the silver mirror which stood behind his wife, and saw there a face that he did not recognize, the face of a stranger, wretched, unhappy.

"Devoured by rats, mired in mud."

London, Palace of Whitehall
17 May 1536

The bells rang to call the Court to evening prayers at Compline. They all made their way towards the Chapel Royal, the ceiling of which was coloured like an azure sky, studded with stars. The sound of the psalm rose in the nave: 'The Lord is My Shepherd… He pastures me in green fields and leads me to calm waters… He guides me along the right path… If I should walk in a dark valley, I shall not be afraid because You are with me.'

Sir Robert watched his people, absorbed as they were in prayer, as if hearing their silent words: 'Save her, Lord. Show us the right way.' He reflected: 'All three of them are desperate to save a life. Lord, help them. It's true: perhaps there is something more important even than justice, that matters more.' He prayed: 'O Lord, in this moment when nothing is clear to me, take my hand, guide me on your path.'

On returning to Sir Robert's rooms, Philip was about to bid the others goodnight, but was invited to remain for a moment. Sir Robert began walking up and down, his face drawn, his hand passing continually through his dishevelled hair. Again Philip wanted to say something, but Lady Constance, finger on lips, signalled to him to keep quiet.

Her husband came up to her and took her hand. "Connie, you know that I am not a courageous man. But if I have said no, it is because of the danger that we would all be running, including that girl. All condemned to become skeletons in some dungeon, eaten alive by rats, drowning in filth."

With an expression of great sadness, he added: "For many days and nights I have been in turmoil, for myself, for you all. I have been afraid. And what's more: dismayed, for having involved you in this business."

Again Philip was on the point of speaking, but was again silenced by a glance from Lady Constance.

"But I was watching you while you were praying. I realized how much more generous you are than I. I have prayed too. After days of agonizing, I think it has become clear to me, I have come to see things in a new light. With regards to Lady Alice in particular: not a murderer, but a human being already treated harshly by life. If she has killed, she only did it to defend herself from the assault of a coward, and she now wishes to provide for Philip's future, her final gift."

He looked each one of them in the face, one by one, to be sure that they understood the significance of what he was saying.

"In short, listen: I have some money here in London, with a merchant banker, Sir Thomas Gresham, an honest man. His father and mine were like brothers. I shall go and see him tomorrow morning. He'll get someone that he trusts to negotiate passage on a ship bound for the Low Countries, and he'll ensure that the gaolers at Newgate get money enough to let Alice escape. With the bank acting as guarantor, it will be as good as done. No-one, and I repeat, no-one will ever know that we were behind the venture."

The others held their breath.

"They will go on board the ship under false names. Sir Thomas' parish priest, who is a trusted friend, will provide the papers for the French parish where they will eventually take refuge. Sir Thomas will be in a position to send them money. We too will be able to keep in touch through his people."

Visibly moved, the two women watched as Sir Robert and Philip embraced each other and parted for the night."

Rendezvous at Billingsgate

London
18 May 1536

On the morning of the eighteenth of May the banker's man went to make arrangements with the master of the *Morning Star* for two passengers on board his ship. It was a fine merchant vessel with large sails and rounded sides, which, after calling at The Hague, would head for France. The ship, anchored downstream from London Bridge at the Billingsgate wharf, would be leaving at sunrise, after the tolling of the bells which announced Prime.

"Passage for two people, and rendezvous at Billingsgate, then," the master had said, pleased with the agreed sum.

"Rendezvous at Billingsgate, downstream from London Bridge," the banker's man had confirmed.

Meanwhile Sir Thomas Gresham went in person to Newgate Prison, paid both the gaoler and the captain of the guards in gold coin, and by means of an order to pay drawn on his own bank, undertook to pay an equal amount when the business was safely concluded

– his correspondents in The Hague would confirm when this had been done.

"And if something goes wrong? If the money doesn't arrive?" Scarcliff had asked.

"Be assured, if something were to go wrong and the money didn't arrive, I personally would pay you, in gold coin."

"All agreed, sir," said the foul-smelling captain. "At dawn tomorrow, when the bells for Prime sound, from here I, Thomas Scarcliff, will take the lady down to the river, to Blackfriars. From there she'll be taken by boat to the mooring stage by the Old Swan, upstream of London Bridge. There will be anchored the *Morning Star*, which will take her on board together with another person."

"Rendezvous at the Old Swan wharf, then, upstream from London Bridge," repeated the banker, and he left for the City and his own bank in Lombard Street.

Before arriving there, though, he paid a visit to the rector of St Mary-le-Bow in Cheapside, who depended greatly on his offerings for the poor: "Dear friend, I need you to insert two baptisms in your parish records – for 1516 and 1517, in the May of those years. It won't hurt anyone, and will certainly do good to many."

"The names, Sir Thomas?"

"A boy." He thought of Philip's initials, Philip Glover, P.G. Let us call him Piers Goldsmith. And a girl, with the initials A.W, Alice Winters. So, let us call her Anne Wentworth."

In the dim light of the vestry the priest pulled off the shelf a dusty tome, marked with the years 1516 and 1517 on its brown vellum spine. He opened it, and leaning over, wrote there what he had been asked. In this way Alice Winter and Philip Glover would have a vital document, a record of baptism, and with this could be obtained a marriage licence in these names. 'Why all this?' he wondered.

Nightmares

London, Palace of Whitehall, Newgate Prison
18 May 1536

Lying in her bed, Margery was not able to sleep. 'I'm old,' she was thinking, 'full of fear, of gloomy premonitions. I am like one of those people who can sense a storm coming, who feel it in the air. Sir Robert says that I am odd, but I scent it, danger. And tomorrow is Friday, the accursed day.'

Indeed, in the space of a month in their lives, a man had been bludgeoned to death, a Queen condemned to the scaffold and their new friend, Alice, shut up in a filthy gaol. What else would happen? And France, so far away, on the other side of the sea: they would lose those children for ever.

While Sir Robert was sleeping, snoring as always when he lay flat out on his back, Lady Constance did not manage to go to sleep. She rose from the bed, opened the shutters and looked out of the window. It was teeming with rain: dark, not a voice to be heard. She seemed to hear the sound of the river, which was growing swollen, or perhaps it was the beating of the rain, or the wind in the trees. A storm, flashes of lightning in the sky, peals of thunder one after the other. And the next day Alice and Philip would be fleeing: she, safe from the gallows, he, forever suspected of loving a murderer. Then, when love finishes: because it always ends, they say…

All of a sudden a cold moon appeared from behind a cloud, lighting up the room. She shivered, pulled her shawl closely around her and went back to bed.

Philip fell asleep immediately, but soon his dream became a nightmare. Margery was talking to him, but her face was that of the seer of Southwark. 'Blood, pools of blood' muttered the woman. 'Death by water' she kept saying. They were in their house at Cambridge, there was blood on the floor in the cellar below. Now the room was full of water, with debris floating in it. Crouched on a table as on a raft, Sir Robert was examining the body of Crooks. But Crooks stood up, walked towards them, holding out his hands, his head a mass of pulp. The old woman of Southwark was laughing, then her face turned into a skull.

He woke up with a cry. It had only been dream, tomorrow they would be escaping to France. He would wait for her on the quay, beside the ship, would help her along the shaky gangplank, as on that day of the trip on the Thames: it was the end of April and he was falling in love.

With the payment of Sir Robert's money, Lady Alice's conditions had changed for the better: no longer

buried in 'the pit', but kept with two other women in a cell with nearly clean straw, a blanket, and the clothes and food which Margery had brought, and which she shared with the others. High up there was a small window with thick rusty bars, and from this a little light filtered down inside. Carved with a nail on the stone walls were some writings – among the many women who had passed through this prison there were some who had known how to write:
'Ruth Gavell 20 years old today'
'Bridget 1512'
'I go to die pray for me'
'I tore the pig to pieces – he deserved it'

Now Lady Alice was sleeping on the straw, curled up under the blanket. That afternoon Philip had seemed excited over something which he had not wanted to tell her about. He had stayed for a long time sitting next to her on the floor. Now in her dreams she saw him as she had always imagined him: a slim handsome face, a youthful beard on his chin, and they were walking together, hand in hand, along an embankment, bathed in moonlight. 'To behold again for a moment the beauty of the world. To succeed in forgetting the past, the painful memory of her mother and father. To manage to forgive herself for being the only survivor. To have hope rekindle' she had thought on waking with a start.

"I have come here to die..."

London, the Tower
19 May 1536

On the seventeenth of May, the same day as the trial of Lady Alice, from her room in the Tower Anne Boleyn saw her own brother George ascend the scaffold.

George was younger than her, and tall, with a thick mass of curly hair and bright azure eyes. Their growing up together at Hever Castle had created a special bond between the two of them. Now, among the pretexts invented to provide grounds for condemning her to death, there was that of incest. After the terrible miscarriage, Crooks had had suspicions and had confronted her one morning: 'I can ruin you,' he had said. Someone had silenced him for good, whoever it was, so he hadn't been there to testify at the trial: all the same, George had been found guilty. Now it was her turn.

At dawn on Friday the nineteenth of May, the Queen heard Mass and took Communion, then awaited the arrival of the Keeper of the Tower, Sir William

Kingston. He arrived soon after. "It is time," he said to her. "I am ready," she replied.

Dressed in a grey damask robe edged with fur, under an ermine-lined coat, her hair gathered up simply beneath a headdress of black velvet decorated with pearls, Anne Boleyn crossed the Great Hall for the last time and walked alongside the west wall of the White Tower, towards the scaffold covered in dark cloth. Kingston offered her his arm as she climbed the steps. She barely spoke to those involved, anxious not to say anything which might offend the King and put little Elizabeth in danger. "I have come here to die," she said, "pray for me."

A witness stated that while she was approaching the block, 'she had never looked so beautiful'.

One of her ladies removed her coat, another undid her hair and helped her tuck it under the special cap used for executions, making sure that it was properly gathered up so as not to impede the headsman's work. She made a gift of her precious Book of Hours to her friend, Lady Margaret Lee, who was beside her; she knelt down in front of the block, laid her head there, opened her arms to signal that she was ready. She murmured "Lord have mercy on me, Jesus save me, Jesus save me!"

Then, with a single stroke of his sword, the executioner cut off her head, which rolled away in the straw; he picked it up by the hair, with blood dripping from the neck, to show it to those assembled, as custom demanded. Afterwards, what remained of her was wrapped up in a white cloth and placed in an old oak chest which had once contained arrows, and left in the chapel of St Peter-in-Chains, inside the Tower. The next day she would be buried in the chapel in an unmarked grave.

A cannon-shot from the Tower announced to the city of London that Anne Boleyn's life had come to an end.

That same day, also at dawn, the gaoler Thomas Scarcliff left Newgate Prison with two oars over his shoulder, leading Lady Alice by the hand. He had allowed her to wash – his wife had come to the gaol for this – and put on clean clothes, and now the morning light accentuated her pale beauty.

"Where are you taking me?" she asked: in fact Sir Robert had asked Philip not to reveal their plans to her for fear that she might betray herself.

"There is a ship waiting for you at the moorings by the Old Swan," replied Thomas. "We'll get in my boat and I shall row you there. And there you will find someone who will look after you."

'Philip,' she thought, 'Philip: you ought not to have done this.'

The sky was clear; the morning air caressed her face. They made their way down alleyways as yet still asleep, along the cobbles of Newgate Street and past the shops on St Andrew's Hill, which still had their shutters closed. There were few people around. They continued beyond Blackfriars Priory, where the first light of the rising sun sparkled through the leaves on the trees.

They arrived at steps on the riverside, where a boat was moored.

"Be careful," said the man, "the river is high after all the rain." He removed the oilcloth covering, wiped up the wet patches on the seat in the prow and settled the young woman. He slid the oars into the row-locks, and untied the boat, which slipped quickly away on the fast-flowing river. On the left-hand bank, down towards London Bridge, the city displayed a skyline of domes, church spires and mansions. As they passed by the different buildings which lined the water's edge, he told her their various names: 'Baynard's Castle', the seat of the Yorks. And here the houses of the guilds: the builders, the glaziers; here the vintners, the joiners."

Her hands resting on the wooden gunwales, Lady Alice listened to him, aware of the sound of the water passing under the keel, and breathing in the fresh smell of the river. She did not respond to the gaoler's words, she was exhausted: she had been tremendously distressed at learning of Crook's death. Her decision not to plead innocent, as all those at Newgate did, had been hard to bear, and the days in prison had been harrowing. She was frightened, felt that punishment was imminent, and set her lips tightly in order to stop herself from crying.

"Just after the Dyers' House, a little before London Bridge, we'll find the moorings at the Old Swan," said the man. But when they arrived at the landing-stage, the ship, the *Morning Star*, wasn't there for the rendezvous.

Philip had been waiting for some considerable time at Billingsgate wharf, under the side of the *Morning Star*. He had arrived long before the agreed hour and had had them load on board the trunk which Lady Constance and Margery had prepared for them. He was carrying with him a purse of money – Sir Robert had been generous – and some letters of credit issued by Sir Thomas Gresham in favour of Piers Goldwell and Anne Wentworth: Londoners, baptized in the parish of St Mary-le-Bow. From Le Havre, where Gresham had a contact, they would head towards a French village inland, seeking shelter for the night in monasteries.

"Over there they are still good Christians," Margery had sighed.

They would start a new life.

But it was now nearly Terce. Alice's boat should have been here some time ago: why was it delayed? The master had been clear, in a little while the ship would have to leave. Philip was seized by a vague uneasiness. Why had Alice been so elusive? It almost seemed as if she wished to punish herself. But at the same time, if she were guilty, it was because she had had to defend herself. Guilty before man, perhaps even in her own eyes, but innocent before God...

Meanwhile the sun had risen, the crossing promised to be easy. Philip peered up the river, but there was no boat in sight. Then, suddenly, the sound of a cannon. 'Anne Boleyn's life has ended,' he thought.

A fatal misunderstanding

London, Billingsgate wharf
19 May 1536

"We shall find the *Morning Star* just after the Dyers' House," Scarcliff had said as he rowed Lady Alice down the river. But of the large ship with the white sails there was no trace.

The man secured his boat on a mooring ring at the Old Swan and helped the young lady out. "I'll go and make some enquiries, don't move from here," he said. "Do you wish to refresh yourself a little? I'll help you down to the water. Here you are."

Then he ran up the steps from the landing-stage and disappeared into the river wardens' hut.

"The *Morning Star*?" an officer replied. "No, it doesn't berth here, it's not deep enough. It'll be at Billingsgate wharf, be assured, down below the Bridge."

"But the rendezvous was here, at the Old Swan moorings: above, I tell you, not below, the Bridge."

"It's not possible, you must have made a mistake," the man said.

In the meantime Alice, having left her shoes on the planks of the prow, took a few steps along the slippery stones of the embankment. A sprightly breeze arose from the river: she relished the air on her face, she wanted to try the freshness of the water. She gathered up her dress, put one foot forward, then the other. Close to the bank the river was calm; she could not know that a little further out it was running more strongly. She took a few more steps, then slipped: no cry, nobody heard or saw anything. She did not realize that the current was pushing her out towards the centre of the river and she stayed still, lying on her back, her arms spread out, as the sun sparkled on her golden hair.

When she arrived under the Tower, just next to Traitors' Gate, through which many innocents had passed on the way to their deaths, she was startled by a deafening blast, the chilling roar of a cannon. And it was in that moment that a flash of light pierced her eyes, shattering her world of shadows: after years spent in darkness, she suddenly beheld white clouds scudding across the sky, yellow irises fringing the river bank, the glistening of the silver water, like lights hanging in the air. She was stunned, overwhelmed. 'To be able to join the living again,' she thought. 'To see Philip's face, his expression, his hands. A life of happiness at his side.' The two of them, and the children that would come. Sweet France, with its luminous skies.

Then, unexpectedly, she was gripped by a feeling of intense horror, of inexpressible anguish: in an instant she relived her whole life, the happy years, the days of the shadows, in a flash she travelled through her memories. What right had she to continue living, how could she still laugh, love and be happy with that sense of remorse which she carried within her? And to have escaped death that day in the woods: she, she alone. And, almost as a punishment, to have killed a man. She saw herself again on that dark night: his disgusting body next to hers, she grasping the candlestick, striking out madly, he collapsing, she trying to rouse him: but the man was dead. She felt soiled by the blood on her hands and in her mind.

As the river carried her further downstream, her bright vision of future happiness gave way to dismay: how long would Philip's love last when he had finally become certain that she was a killer? When would he stop loving her? One morning she would awake and read it in his eyes.

A new thought crossed her mind: 'To pass into the hereafter, to escape the bondage of suffering, the parched thirsts of summer and the storms of winter' as her nurse used to sing. 'To fear no more the unburied phantoms. To come to a safe haven, to reach home, at the end of the road. To enter into a world of peace, into a new kind of joy.'

It was in that moment that she stopped struggling. The clouds covered the sun, the river wrapped her round like a cloak, and her clothes, weighed down by the water, pulled her into the depths.

They found her further downstream, the morning after, near Greenwich, on a bend where the current is gentle.

Epilogue

England, thirty years later

When free of Anne Boleyn, **King Henry VIII** married Lady Jane Seymour, and when she died he married three more times. He divorced his fourth wife, the ungainly Anne of Cleves, sent to the block his fifth one, the young Kathryn Howard, who had been unfaithful. The sixth, Katharine Parr, survived him.

Early in his reign, an old woman condemned to the gallows had raised her arm at him and shouted: "Henry, you too will die, and dogs shall lick your blood." Years later, during his funeral, the coffin had split open, blood had run out and two huge black dogs, which seemed to have come from Hell itself, had leapt forward to lap it up.

The Duke of Norfolk, prisoner in the Tower, only survived because the King died a few hours before signing the order for his execution. After a life full of cruelty and the abuse of power, he changed his religion and became a Catholic. This secured his pardon from Queen Mary Tudor, the Catholic daughter of Henry and Katharine of Aragon, and he died peacefully in his bed.

As for **Elizabeth (Bessie) Holland**, when her lover the Duke of Norfolk was sent to the Tower, she testified against him, revealing the extent of his misdeeds. Immediately afterwards she married Henry Reppes whom she had long loved, but died in childbirth the same year.

At the fall of the Duke of Norfolk, **Sir Nicholas Sherman** took refuge in France. Sir Robert Kytchyn never found out whether his friend had really betrayed his trust.

The poet **Sir Thomas Wyatt** was released from the Tower thanks to his family's influence with Sir Thomas Cromwell, the King's Chancellor. From the window of his cell, it is likely that he witnessed the beheading of the alleged lovers of the Queen, and of the Queen herself, whom he had always loved.

The young **Philip Glover** returned to Cambridge and to the house of Sir Robert and Lady Constance, became a capable doctor and thirty years later, his hair already turning grey, was appointed Master of Pembroke College. He married a young woman from Norfolk, a grand-niece of Margery Ackworth, and with her had several children: the first, a baby girl 'with golden hair and eyes a deep blue like the sky on certain summer days', he chose to call Alice.

Characters

Anne Boleyn (c. 1501 or 1505 – 19 May 1536), second wife and queen consort of King Henry VIII, and mother of the future Queen Elizabeth I. Accused of adultery and incest, she was beheaded in the Tower of London. "She was very beautiful, she had dark eyes and hair, a slim figure, a slender neck and an elegance acquired at the court of France."

Elizabeth (Bessie/Bess) Holland (? – 1547), former mistress of Thomas Howard, third Duke of Norfolk. "A commoner of striking beauty, with a head of red curly hair, a turned-up nose and a contagious laugh."

George Boleyn (c.1504 – 17 May 1536), brother of Queen Anne Boleyn, who supported his rise to power. Accused of incest with his sister, he was beheaded on 17 May 1536. "Younger than her, tall, with curly hair and eyes of a bright sky blue."

Henry VIII (1491 – 1547), King of England and Lord of Ireland and the Islands. Married six times, he broke with the Church of Rome. In order to marry Anne

Boleyn, he put away his first wife, Catherine of Aragon, who died of grief in a remote castle.

As a young man hailed as 'the handsomest prince in Christendom', he became "an obese tyrant, his face swollen, his stomach mountainous, one leg covered in sores and threatening to turn gangrenous...".

Lady Alice Winter, maid of honour to Queen Anne Boleyn, and under her protection since becoming an orphan at seventeen years of age. "She was tall, slim, with gentle features, soft blond hair arranged discreetly, eyes of a dark blue seen on certain days in summer."

Lady Constance, wife of Sir Robert Kytchyn. "She was taller than her husband, her eyes green flecked with gold, a strong nose, a resolute stance, graceful in her cream-coloured brocaded dress, with a head-dress the same flame-red colour as her hair."

Lady Margaret Lee (1506? – 43?), friend and confidante of Queen Anne Boleyn. "She was tall, with a sharp nose and thin lips, set in hard face."

Margery Ackworth, governess to Lady Constance. "It was difficult to say how old Margery was: the woman was strong, energetic, skilled at washing with cinders. She had bright cheeks in a ruddy face, with fine veins under pale-blue eyes. Only the gnarled hands and the odd grey curl which escaped from under her bonnet betrayed her real age." She had raised the little Constance from the moment that the child had lost her mother, had taught her how to behave and to write a few words, before her father engaged a tutor for her. When Constance, now a young lady, had gone to Court, Margery had followed, as she had when Constance married: from that time she had extended her affection to Sir Robert, helping him when he had difficulties in his investigations. For she, with her maternal air, was able to glean from anyone their most intimate secrets, which she then passed to him.

Philip Glover, assistant to Sir Robert Kytchyn, "was a tall, slender youth, with a clear complexion, eyes the colour of light chestnut, and the carefully tended beginnings of a beard. Studious, but also a dreamer – he plays the lute, composes songs."

Simon Barefoot, assistant to the court doctor. "He is one of those whose origins are not clear, certainly not Oxford. He has the bland eloquence of the prelate, and people are deceived by him, but he conceals a knife beneath his cassock."

Sir Nicholas Sherman, gentleman of the Bedchamber to Thomas Howard, third Duke of Norfolk. "Since his time at Cambridge he had been tall and well-built, but had now grown more solid, and his face had become hard, as if carved in wood. For some time in the service of the Duke, he had fought with him against the Scots and acted as ambassador on several missions."

Sir Robert Kytchyn, Dean of Pembroke College, Cambridge, doctor and coroner, charged by the King with the inquest into the death of William Crooks. "He is a man of about forty, with some marks of age on his lively face, his hair already grey and always ruffled, a bulge developing around his waist, and small horn-rimmed glasses before his blue eyes giving him the appearance of an owl."

Sir Thomas Wyatt (1503-1542), poet. Accused of being one of the lovers of Queen Anne Boleyn, with whom he was secretly in love, he was imprisoned in the Tower in May 1536. "He was in his thirties, tall, strong, his eyes a misty grey and his hair red. A comely face, interesting."

Sir William Brereton (c. 1490 — 17 May 1536), **Sir Henry Norris** (1490 – 17 May 1536), **Sir Francis Weston** (1511 – 17 May 1536), **Mark Smeaton** (c. 1518 – 17 May 1536), were the alleged lovers of Queen Anne Boleyn, for which charge they were condemned to death. They ascended the scaffold two days before their queen.

Thomas Howard, third Duke of Norfolk (1473 – 1554), uncle of two of Henry VIII's wives. Cruel and unscrupulous, he was imprisoned in the Tower following the downfall of his niece Kathryn. The king's sudden death saved him from execution for high treason.

William Crooks, personal servant to Queen Anne Boleyn and placed in this position by the King in order to spy on her movements. "A man of about forty, short of stature, heavily built, a great eater and drinker, his forehead low, with thick eyebrows, a broad nose, fleshy lips, a double chin, broken teeth, his few hairs reddish in colour."

Places

Cambridge. The delightful county town of Cambridgeshire is located 60 miles north-east of London. It is the site of a very old university: in 1209, in fact, some scholars fleeing from Oxford on account of disputes with the local citizens, found refuge at Cambridge and there established a new seat of learning. Pembroke College, which is mentioned in the story, was founded in 1347 by Marie de St Pol, Countess of Pembroke.

Hampton Court. The restoration of the 'Court of Hampton', a few miles from London, was begun in 1514 by the then archbishop and Chancellor of King Henry VIII Thomas Wolsey, who transformed it into a magnificent residence in the Tudor style. The archbishop rebuilt the splendid house, which – with its distinctive red bricks – stood out amidst rich green fields and gardens; he had the great hall done in the mediaeval fashion, long and high, with luminous stained-glass windows, the walls hung with sumptuous tapestries, and dominating all, a throne on which to receive kings and ambassadors. He erected the imposing Royal Chapel, with its sky-blue ceiling

214

depicting a starry sky, the huge cellars for the vintage wines which arrived from all over Europe, and the kitchens with their enormous chimneys, which could serve more than a thousand guests at a sitting.

A short while before being found guilty of treason, Wolsey sought to ward off the King's anger by making him a gift of this luxurious complex.

The Tower. This is the name by which the Tower of London is known, in its time fortress, gunpowder magazine, royal residence, prison for the high-born and sinister place of torture for ordinary subjects of the realm. Its history began around 1070 when William the Conqueror (1066-87) started its construction. Such a wonder had never before been seen: the building (the White Tower) was immense, being 36 metres high and 32 metres wide, and dominated all of mediaeval London. It was surrounded by fortified walls, and over the centuries other structures were added, each one bearing the mark of whichever monarch had been at work.

Whitehall Palace. This assemblage of buildings is located near Westminster, on the northern banks of the River Thames. Cardinal Wolsey took up residence there and carried out extensive renovations: large libraries, collections of paintings, rich furnishing of gold and precious stones, apartments with tapestries interwoven with gold. The King seized possession of it and made it his London residence when Wolsey fell into disgrace in 1529.

Hever Castle, in the rich Kent countryside, was originally a farm belonging to the De Hevere family, granted to them by William the Conqueror. The farm was converted into a manor house by Anne Boleyn's great-grandfather, Geoffrey Bullen, Lord Mayor of London, and this was where Anne Boleyn spent her childhood.

The castle is an outstandingly handsome Tudor mansion, with surrounding walls and a double moat, and with some of the most attractive gardens in England. Inside can be found portraits of Anne Boleyn and Henry VIII. In Anne's room, which is situated on the top floor of the building, is preserved a Book of Hours which belonged to her.

Primary and secondary sources

Ackroyd, Peter, *Londra, Biografia di una città*, Frassinelli, Milano **2004**

Baskerville, **Geoffrey,** *English Monks and the Suppression of the Monasteries*, Yale University Press, New Haven, N.J., **1937**

Brewer, J.S. , Gairdner, James, Brodie, **R.H.** eds., *Letters and Papers, Foreign and Domestic, in the Reign of Henry VIII*, H.M.S.O., London **1864- 1910**

Cressy, **David,** *Birth, Marriage and Death: Ritual Religions and the Life-Cycle in Tudor and Stuart England*, Oxford University Press, Oxford **1977**

Doner, **Margaret,** *Lies and Lust in the Tudor Court, The Fifth Wife of Henry VIII*, iUniverse, Inc., New York - Lincoln - Shanghai, **2004**

Elton, **G. R. ,***The Tudor Constitution: Documents and Commentary*, Cambridge University Press, Cambridge **1960**

Erickson, **Carolly,** *Il grande Harry*, Arnoldo Mondadori Editore, Milano **1980/2002**

Fletcher, **Anthony,** *Tudor Rebellions,* Longman, London **1968**

Fraser, **Antonia,** *The Six Wives of Henry VIII,* **1992** George Weidenfeld & Nicolson Ltd; **2002** Phoenix Press Orion Books Ltd, Orion House 5 Upper St

Martin's Lane, London WC2H 9EA; *Le sei mogli di Enrico VIII,* Mondadori, Milano, **1995**

George, **Margaret,** *The Autobiography of Henry VIII,* St.Martin's Press, 175 Fifth Avenue, New York, N.Y: 10010, **1986;** *Il re e il suo giullare,* TEADUE, Milano **1995**

Guy, **John,** *Tudor England,* Oxford University Press, London **1988**

Hall, **Edward,** *Chronicle Containing the History of England,* J. Johnson, London **1809**

Hanson, **Marilee,** *Tudor England, 1485-1603,* "*Letters of the Six Wives of Henry VIII*" (download: http://englishhistory.net/tudor.html)

Herbert, Edward, 1st Baron of Cherbury, *The Life and Reign of King Henry VIII,* Andrew Clark, London **1672**

Ives, **Eric W.** ,*The Life and Death of Anne Boleyn,* Blackwell Publishing Ltd, Oxford **2004**

Lindsey, **Karen.** *Divorced, Beheaded, Survived,* Da Capo Press, Cambridge, Massachusetts, **1995**

Moberly, **Charles Edward,** *Henry VIII King of England, 1491-1547,* C.Scribner's Sons, **1906**

Moretti, Mariella, *Caterina d'Aragona, Anna Bolena, Jane Seymour, Anna di Cleves, Kathryn Howard, Katharine Parr, Maria I (Bloody Mary), Margaret Beaufort, Elizabeth Blount, Anne Neville,* Enciclopedia delle donne, Milano**,** 2017/2022

Mumby, **Frank Arthur,** *The Youth of Henry VIII, A Narrative in Contemporary Letters,* Houghton Miffling Company, Boston & New York, **1913**

Picard, Liza, *Elizabeth's London,* St.Martin's Press, New York **2003**

Plowden, Alison, *Tudor Women, Queens & Commoners,* **1979** Weidenfield & Nicolson; **2007** Sutton Publishing Ltd, Stroud, Gloucestershire

Pollard, Albert Frederick, *Henry VIII,* Longmans Green & Co., London **1905/1951**

Ridgway, Claire, *The Fall of Anne Boleyn, A Countdown,* **2012**; *The Real Truth about the Tudors,* The Anne Boleyn Collection, **2012**; *Sweating Sickness in a Nutshell,* **2014**; *Tudor Places of Great Britain,* **2015**; *On This Day in Tudor History,* **2015**. Made Global Publishing, both Paperback and Kindle Editions.

Sansom, C.J., *Dissolution, A Novel of Tudor England,* Penguin Group, 80 Strand, London **2003**

Sansom, C.J., *Sovereign,* Macmillan **2006**, poi Pan Macmillan, London **2007 - 2008**

Sansom, C.J., *Dark Fire,* Penguin Group, 80 Strand, London, **2004**

St Clare Byrne, **Muriel,** editor, *The Lisle Letters,* Penguin Books, Harmondsworth, Middlesex, England, **1983**

Stow, John, *A Survey of London,* London **1598**. Reissued by Sutton Publishing, Stroud, Glos., 1997

Warnicke, **Retha M. ,** *The Rise and Fall of Anne Boleyn,* Cambridge University Press, Cambridge **1989 – 1991**

Weir, **Alison,** *The Six Wives of Henry VIII,* **1991** The Bodley Head; **1992** Pimlico Edition; **2007** Vintage, Random House, 20 Vauxhall Bridge Road, London SW1V 2SA

Williams, **Neville,** *Henry VIII and His Court*, Macmillan, New York **1971**

Wilson, **Derek,** *In the Lion's Court: Power, Ambition, and Sudden Death in the Reign of Henry VIII,* St. Martin's Press, New York **2002**

Wriothesley, **Charles,** *A Chronicle of England during the Reigns of the Tudors,* from 1485 to 1559, Camden Society, **1885** / Kessinger Publishing Rare Reprints **2007**

Zajde, **Nathalie,** *I figli dei sopravvissuti*, Moretti &Vitali Editori, Bergamo **2002**

About the authors

After completing her studies in Italy and the UK, and after teaching English for several years, **Mariella Moretti** moved to work in the field of applied linguistics. For a number of years she worked in educational publishing, and is currently engaged in the writing of historical fiction, and in the research and study that this involves.

After many years as a teacher of English in a variety of fields, roles and locations, **Colin Sowden** now works as a free-lance examiner, translator and teacher-trainer, with a special interest in course design, materials creation and writing.

Acknowledgements

Mariella Moretti would like to thank Laura Lepri and Bruna Miorelli for their rigorous yet supportive editing, and Lucia Incerti Caselli, Silvia Cutaia, Maria Di Donato, Anna Fassini, Christian Hill, Serena and Domenico Lazzaro, Gabriella Mariano, Chiara Motton, Silvia Penati, Paola Pirzio and Mary Shannon for reviewing the manuscript and for their suggestions.

She is also grateful to all the authors mentioned in the bibliography, and particularly to Peter Ackroyd, Antonia Fraser, Margaret George, Philippa Gregory, Karen Lindsey, Liza Picard, Alison Plowden, Albert Frederick Pollard, C.J.Sansom and Alison Weir.

For their guidance, she thanks again Laura Lepri, Bruna Miorelli, John Gardner, Rhona Martin, Owain Sowden and Sol Stein.

Printed in Great Britain
by Amazon